THE STEWARDESS TO
half-full.

CW00350848

Maybe she'd luck out, herself.

Even as she was letting her hopes rise on that score, someone half-threw their body into the aisle seat closest to hers.

Whoever he was, he was tall, lean, and took up an inordinate amount of space, and not only physically. He sprawled in the seat, legs open, his arms hanging over the seat between them, taking up significantly more than just the armrest on his side. She found herself glad he hadn't been assigned to the middle seat, at least.

At least now, a seat still broke up the space between them.

Even as the thought crossed her mind, he shoved up his inside armrest and slid over into the seat next to hers.

Before she could get over her surprise, he turned, grinning at her.

Staring up at that face, Lia frowned, struck by a vague familiarity—

"Hello, gorgeous," he said, grinning wider as he stared into her eyes. "I'd like my ring back now. If it's all the same to you."

Those leaf-green eyes turned a touch harder, even as his grin widened.

"*Right* now," he said, speaking through that smile.

LOKI

Gods on Earth #2

JC ANDRIJESKI

Loki (Gods on Earth #2)

Copyright 2021 by JC Andrijeski

Published by White Sun Press

First Edition

ISBN: 9798723850460

Cover Art & Design by Sylvia Frost of The Book Brander (2020)

This book is licensed for your personal enjoyment only. All rights reserved.
This is a work of fiction. All characters and events portrayed in this book are
fictional, and any resemblance to real people, organizations or events is
purely coincidental. This book, or parts thereof, may not be reproduced in
any form without permission.

Link with me at: https://jcandrijeski.com

Or at: https://www.facebook.com/groups/thelightsanctuary

Mailing List: https://bit.ly/JCA-mail

White Sun Press

Printed in the United States of America 2021

THIEF

He barely noticed the nudge.

The physical contact slid past his awareness without him registering more than a faint brush of fingers, hardly unusual in a crowded market in this part of the world.

Kathmandu, Nepal, with its surrounding Himalayan mountain range, endless temples and shrines for multiple religions and sects, lax borders, bribe-able officials, and crowded streets, tons of outdoor markets and side alleys and tucked-away restaurants and coffee gardens, was a mass of discordant humanity, in all of its fetid, colorful, chaotic glory.

Loki came here to disappear.

For the same reason, he was far more concerned someone might recognize *him* than he was about any other person who might be trying to move through the crowd unseen.

Then he noticed his hands.

One hand, in particular.

"Odin's hairy asshole... what in the seven *hells!*" The god sputtered the words in the Asgardian tongue, earning him a few puzzled looks, but no comprehension.

Loki scarcely favored them with a glance.

He spun around where he stood, using his significant height to scan the crowd, even as he rolled back his god's photographic memory, looking for the *exact moment,* the *precise touch* or brush of fingers from the *exact person or persons* standing or walking anywhere near him in the period directly before he noticed his ring missing.

He found the instant he felt that bare nudge, that feather-like brush of fingers.

He saw her, in his mind's eye.

Her appearance paralyzed him briefly.

One might even say it shocked him.

Long, thick blond hair, full, pert lips, green, cat-like eyes, a calf-length coat made of dark green leather that matched those eyes, a turquoise pendant around her neck next to an older, beat-up, silver ring looped around the same chain. Furred boots. A leather satchel worn crosswise over her body. Big tits. Small waist. Long, muscular legs.

High cheekbones. Intelligent eyes.

If he'd been in a different world, he might have thought her an elf.

A dickish elf.

A very hot, sexy, dickish elf.

One he very much intended to find.

Once he'd nailed down the physical ID, he pulled himself out of his recollection and scanned the crowd a second time, looking for the woman he'd seen behind his eyes.

Luckily, in this part of the world, blond hair still stood out.

His elfin thief hadn't worn a hat, so he was able to spot her, even as she was about to turn the corner into a side alley.

Loki pushed his way through the crowd, fighting a clear path through the street lined on both sides with market stalls, about half of them selling crap, maybe a third selling food, and the rest selling things that could actually be considered of worth, from a human standpoint, at least. He came close to knocking over two locals in his haste, one carrying an enormous pack filled with hand-woven blankets, and the other pushing a cart filled with bread, cheeses, and what looked like small sausages.

Loki barely gave them a look as they each yelled at him in their local tongue, complaining and cursing loudly as they shook their fists.

He threw a coin at the one with the bread, since he knocked down a few loafs, muttering a few words in Nepalese as he passed.

"Tut-tut, gentleman... lady... but I'm faced with a far more important errand than either of you. One where your *own, small, petty human world* may very well hang in the balance. Truly, your destinies might currently reside in the sticky, greedy hands of a sexy, dickish elf with stunning eyes and absolutely enormous tits..."

Loki darted between and around thickly-dressed bodies, their clothes and shopping bags and wheeled carts filling the narrow street, along with rusted motorcycles, pastel-colored scooters, auto-rickshaws, the occasional car, the occasional cow, the occasional monkey.

Loki didn't let himself get distracted.

His eyes remained transfixed on the mouth of the alley where he'd last seen her.

He remained so focused on his destination, he didn't pay enough attention to closer by and plowed into a lowing ox being ushered down the street by a small, impossibly-ancient Tibetan woman, who dressed the ox in colorful blankets and jangly head-gear.

Loki managed to get around the domestic creature only to be nearly struck down a second time by a kid on a battered moped, who cursed at him in Hindi and flipped the god off for his trouble.

Loki didn't bother to return the insult.

He reached the mouth of the alley a few seconds later, and skidded sideways at the mouth before regaining his traction and darting inside.

He came to a dead stop, looking around with a frown when it was empty.

The alley snaked in a curving path, a path made of cobblestones and packed dirt. Baskets hung outside one of the homes, with hanging tapestries in the doors of others, a kind of make-shift screen used to air out houses in this part of the world, and keep some of the bugs at bay.

Loki jogged warily down the passage, listening to sounds from the dwellings on either side. He saw birds in cages outside several doors, laundry hanging in the cold sunshine, a boy toddler playing in a basin of water with only a T-shirt and no pants, his tiny penis flopping up and down as he jumped and splashed in delight.

No blond thief.

No green leather coat.

No satchel likely containing his ring.

A ring he worked *far too hard* to come into possession of.

That same ring formed a good chunk of the reason he was stuck in this hell-hole in the first place. And the irony was, the ring, apart from being a pretty bauble, was entirely useless to the human who'd stolen it.

It only held real value for an immortal, like him.

Loki finally conceded defeat after he'd traversed a few hundred yards down the alley.

Coming to another dead stop, he looked back and forth in either direction.

The minx had given him the slip.

He would have to find her another way.

꧁ꕥ꧂

He poured out a handful of coins on top of the donation plate, his pale, new-leaf-colored eyes boring into the old man's dark brown ones.

After he'd dumped out the money, Loki tossed down a drawing he'd done by hand, using his god's memory, a ballpoint pen he'd purchased for a few Nepalese rupees, and a skill he'd acquired through years of boredom in Asgardian cells. He placed the blue-ink sketch on top of the money, which was three times what the old monk usually charged.

Loki was a god.

He knew which of these creatures were charlatans, and which genuinely had the sight.

He'd walked down the back alleys of the monk's areas near the largest temple, poking his head in doorways until he found one of these chanters who could actually see something. This man had the strongest sight of the three Loki found with any vision at all.

Now he sat cross-legged on the floor of the man's tiny apartments, surrounded by the thick smell of burning incense, small altars dedicated to various teachers and devas, a large one devoted to Chenrezig Bodhisattva, copper cups of water and fruit, small postcards showing animal and water spirits next to floating Buddhas in the clouds.

Loki winked at an image of the Green Tara, then aimed his gaze at the old monk.

"Find her for me." The Trickster God didn't voice it as a question, or a request. "Do it quickly, and I'll give you double what is there, old man."

The old monk looked at him warily, almost like he could see Loki for who he was.

"Who is she?" the monk asked.

Wooden prayer beads wound around one of his hands and

wrists. He looked Loki over even more carefully after he voiced his question, seeming to note every aspect of his physical appearance: his long, half-braided, black and auburn hair, his pale eyes, his dark complexion, the smirk on his full lips, the open shirt with the runic tattoos over the top of his chest.

Whatever the old man saw, it didn't reassure him.

The monk's voice grew faintly worried.

"You do not intend to hurt her?" he said. "If I help you find her?"

Loki gave the bald, Nepalese monk in his burgundy and gold robes a wry smile.

"What do you care what I do with her? She's a foreigner. And a thief. I'd bet you wheelbarrows-full of your worthless money she's not a Buddhist... or a very, very bad one."

The monk's mouth grew pinched. "Yes. Perhaps. But you will not—"

"I won't hurt her, old man," Loki said, exhaling his impatience. "I don't kick dogs. I don't hurt dumb beasts. I don't beat on little, blond elves with sticky fingers. She stole something from me. I simply want it back. She's a foreigner, so for all I know she could hop on some rickety, shit-smelling bus with a bunch of other stupid animals, and I'd have to go looking for her in Rishikesh or Agra or Delhi or Varanasi... or some other den of crapulence to the south I'd rather not visit presently. I want to catch her *here*. I want my belonging *back in my possession* before I leave Nepal. Then I will let the little elf go wherever she wishes. Maybe with an imprint of my hand on her ass as a reminder that it's not nice to steal from gods..."

The old monk continued to frown at him, but the worst of his alarm seemed to fade from his eyes. Loki had no idea what conclusions the monk drew from what Loki just said, nor did he care, as long as the monk found his thief.

The old man closed his eyes while Loki watched.

Smoke from incense coiled around the two of them, marking thin, snaking patterns through the already-pungent air.

Loki held himself perfectly still, watching the oracle's face.

He did not have the sight himself, although he could occasionally read minds, like any of the gods. If a connection existed between himself and the mind he intended to read, Loki could at least pick up emotions and intent, if not actual words.

He had no connection to this monk, but something about the process of the human using his gifts allowed Loki to feel a whisper of when it began to work.

Maybe he was simply close enough to pick up a smattering of the images soaked up by the old monk's aura.

Whatever the case, he wasn't surprised when the monk opened his eyes a few beats later.

"You were right to be concerned," the monk said, his voice losing all of its worry and uncertainty, instead sounding resolutely certain. "She is at the airport right now, friend."

"The airport!"

Loki leapt to his feet.

Pausing only long enough to empty more of the rupees in his pockets onto the donation plate of the old monk, he ran out through the hanging tapestry of the multi-headed bodhisattva that fluttered over the monk's front door. Dashing out into the street, Loki looked in either direction frantically before he made out a taxi and waved it down, putting his fingers to his lips and whistling—loudly—to get the driver's attention.

The sound was so piercing, the taxi skidded to a stop.

The driver looked over at him in bewilderment.

Several other humans nearby also winced at the sound,

and now stared at Loki as he darted through traffic, making his way to the battered cab painted all over with the Buddha's eyes of compassion, and an image of Ganesha, the Elephant God.

Ah, Nepal.

Loki did not wait to be invited, but yanked open the back door of the cab.

He dove inside, already speaking to the wide-eyed driver.

"To the airport," Loki demanded, jabbing a finger in the air. "Now. This very instant! And quickly! Drive *very* fast... *dangerously fast*, my good man. Safety last, is what I'm saying. I will reward you handsomely if you get me there in an inhumanly quick amount of time. I will give you a tongue-lashing the entire way there if I don't feel *perilously* close to dying due to your speed and risk-taking on the road..."

The Nepalese taxi driver didn't need any more than that.

There was nothing a Nepalese taxi driver loved better than a promise of money and a dare to get somewhere quicker than any of his brothers.

Smashing his sandaled foot down on the gas pedal, he darted out into the mid-afternoon traffic, leaving a cloud of diesel fumes in his wake.

LIA

Lia sighed, sinking into her assigned airplane seat and tossing her battered leather satchel down on the floor by her feet.

She'd asked for a window seat on her flight back to Los Angeles, and they'd given her one, at least for this first leg of the journey, which would take her to Bangkok, Thailand for a few hours before she boarded the second leg of the flight to California.

Leaning her head back on the cloth seat, she stared up at the small round vents blowing air on her, frowning a little as she reached up to turn them off. She never understood why anyone would want a bunch of freezing cold, stale air blowing on them while they sat on a plane surrounded by strangers.

Finding her seatbelt ends on either side, including the half that was under her butt, she pulled them out and clicked the metal ends together, sighing as she adjusted her back in the cushion. She couldn't always sleep on flights, but she would this time.

Thank goodness for valerian root... and melatonin.

And wine.

Some delicate balancing of the three nearly always did the trick, knocking her out cold for at least five or six hours. She'd turned catching sleep in the odd-hours and minutes into a near art-form in the months she'd been traveling in Asia, which seemed to be happening more and more often lately, since her boss, Gregor Farago, decided to expand his business east.

He'd probably be sending her out here even more in the coming months.

This trip had more been laying the groundwork for that, and for Gregor's negotiations with a particular fat cat oper- ating out of China.

Gregor had been trying to penetrate the guy's inner circle for months, and thanks to Lia, he might finally have enough leverage to do it.

Not like Lia much cared.

She went where she was told. She stole what she was told to steal.

Sometimes she also took a little extra for herself, if the risk seemed small enough.

Gregor didn't exactly pay her, since she was working off dear ol' mom's debt, so it was up to Lia to do what she could on the side. She was trying her damnedest to squirrel away a nest egg for herself and her baby sister, Maia—assuming either of them ever got out from under Gregor's thumb.

As for the work she did for Gregor, Lia no longer asked questions.

She couldn't afford to.

She did as she was told, hoping like hell Gregor would honor their deal, letting her and Maia go once she'd squared things. It had been five years since Lia started working for Gregor, trying to end the nightmare her mother left behind when she stole a chunk of change off Gregor and left Lia and her little sister to pay the tab.

Five long years.

Pushing Gregor out of her mind, Lia refocused on the cabin around her, watching people file onto the plane. She felt a little whisper of relief each and every time new passengers walked past by her row, and especially the two seats adjacent to hers.

The stewardess told her the flight was only about half-full.

Maybe she'd luck out, get her little piece of plane all to herself.

Even as she was letting her hopes rise on that score, someone half-threw their body into the aisle seat closest to hers.

Whoever he was, he was tall, lean, and took up an inordinate amount of space, and not only physically. He sprawled in the seat, legs open, his arms hanging over the seat between them, taking up significantly more than just the armrest on his side. She found herself glad he hadn't been assigned to the middle seat, at least.

At least now, a seat still broke up the space between them.

Even as the thought crossed her mind, he shoved up his inside armrest and slid over into the seat next to hers.

Before she could get over her surprise, he turned, grinning at her.

Staring up at that face, Lia frowned, struck by a vague familiarity—

"Hello, gorgeous," he said, grinning wider as he stared into her eyes. "I'd like my ring back now. If it's all the same to you."

Those leaf-green eyes turned a touch harder, even as his grin widened.

"Right now," he said, speaking through that smile.

Lia felt some of the blood drain from her face.

She remembered him now.

From the market.

She'd noticed him even before she noticed the odd jewelry he wore.

Really, he'd been a veritable treasure-trove of interesting and possibly-valuable looking accessories, from the strange, horned creature he wore in silver around his neck, to the bronze bracelet he wore around one wrist that appeared to have symbols or writing on it from a language she didn't recognize.

Even his body had strange markings on it.

She'd noted what looked like runic tattoos across the top of his chest.

She found herself staring at those tattoos now, black and gold over his darkish skin, nearly at eye-level as he leaned closer.

In the market, she'd settled on just taking his one ring.

She'd viewed it as a token from Kathmandu, where she hadn't had the opportunity to steal much of value, at least not for herself. Perhaps even a token of the man himself, who'd struck her as unique in the sea of bodies wandering through the Kathmandu streets near the old stupas, and not only due to his jewelry.

The ring itself fascinated her.

It seemed to glow from his right hand, where he wore it on his middle digit. It looked like real gold, possibly with some other metal threaded through, and the runes decorating the edge were beautiful, painted deep black and carved with precision.

She was sure Fonzo could unload it for her. He could possibly even sell it at auction, if it turned out to be a genuine antique.

If it turned out to be worth nothing, she'd just keep it herself.

That, or give it to Maia.

Now she found herself staring at the ring's owner, wondering how the hell he'd found her. Truthfully, she hadn't thought he'd even felt her lift the ring. She'd managed it while he'd been staring at a stand covered in statues made of various crystals and quartz.

He hadn't even looked at her as she coaxed it off his finger.

But he must have felt something.

He also must have tailed her, both on foot and in a taxi or auto-rickshaw, and caught up with her at the airport.

Had he really bought a ticket to Los Angeles—or even just to Bangkok—for a stupid ring? Was it the *one ring to rule them all* or something?

Some kind of family heirloom?

Just her luck the stupid thing would actually matter to him this much, that he'd be crazy enough to follow her onto a plane to get it back.

"Excuse me?" Lia gave him her most disarming, blond-girl smile, blanking her eyes. "I'm so sorry, but I think you must have the wrong person."

The leaf-green eyes stared at her.

They didn't so much as flicker.

"No," he said. "I most definitely do not."

Lia pursed her lips, giving him a puzzled look, her eyes still mostly blank.

"I'm sorry," she said, smiling. "I really don't recognize you. You honestly think we've met somewhere before? In Nepal? Or somewhere else?"

"I honestly think you took the ring off my finger in the market like a sneaky little elf," the man replied, his smile unwavering below those hard, sharp-looking eyes. "I honestly think you're a naughty, smirky, unapologetic thief, and an accomplished liar, and I could pick you up and drag you out of here by your hair and no one could stop me."

He paused, still smiling at her.

"Or," he said, tilting his head. "I could simply throttle you with one hand while I search your person... or until you pass out and I can search you more easily."

He paused again.

"Or," he said, smiling a touch wider. "I could grab you by the ankles, hold you up, and shake you... hard... until the ring falls out of whatever crevice or orifice in which you've stashed my shiny, *very important,* little trinket."

Lia blinked, feeling some of the blood drain from her face.

Her jaw hardened then, even as she searched those pale eyes.

She wasn't about to let some bozo with a mental problem take the one item she'd managed to lift all day that might actually be worth something.

"I'm afraid I'm going to have to call the stewardess," she said politely, smiling back at him. "You seem rather unhinged, if you don't mind my saying. I don't really feel safe sitting next to you. I might even have to scream rape. And flash my American passport around a little. And mention to anyone who will listen that my father works at one of the embassies... and therefore I have diplomatic immunity."

That last part wasn't true of course, but her passport said it was.

Just one of the many perks of working for the Syndicate.

Across from her, those green eyes didn't flicker.

He stared at her, his expression unmoving, his mouth still in that disturbing grin.

"I think I can probably scream louder than you," he told her. "I can also make you scream... and the stewardess scream... and possibly the pilot. I don't think you've quite grasped what you're dealing with here, little girl."

Lia quirked an eyebrow, smiling back at him.

"I really don't know what you mean," she said sweetly, pressing the call button subtly with one hand, hiding it from him by shifting sideways in her seat. "But if you need help locating whatever it is you think you lost—"

"I did not *lose* anything, human—"

"Human?" She quirked an eyebrow at him. "Are you a fish?"

The man didn't so much as blink.

"Give it back to me. Now. I will not ask again."

"I would," she said, smiling sympathetically. "I really, really would... but I honestly have no idea what you're talking about, sir..."

She trailed when the stewardess approached their seats, tilting her head sideways in a silent question as she looked between Lia and her new seatmate. The woman stopped at the end of their row, her hands resting easily on top of each aisle seat.

Right as she paused, and before she spoke, the jet's engines revved into a higher-pitched whine, right before the plane started moving backwards. It rolled smoothly away from the terminal and the receding jetway.

"Is there something I can help you with?" the stewardess asked politely. She aimed her stare at Lia, her eyes saying something along the lines of, *if you need help, blink once. If you're okay, blink twice.* "I believe this seat is vacant, sir. Do you want to accompany me to your assigned seat on the plane?"

The man didn't so much as glance at her.

"Give me the ring," he said to Lia, his voice as hard as glass. "Your thievery is losing its charm, girl, clever as it may have been. Give it to me, and all will be well again. I won't even punish you... most likely."

"Sir?" the stewardess said, speaking louder over the plane's engine, leaning her head and part of her upper body down, likely in an attempt to pull his attention to her. "I'm afraid I'm going to have to ask you to return to your assigned seat."

"I cannot return there," the man told her, without looking away from Lia. "As I have never been there." His eyes hardened on Lia's. "Do you want me to hurt the nice lady, thief? Or can we settle this in a civilized manner?"

Lia held up her hands, keeping her eyes totally blank.

"I just haven't the faintest clue what he's talking about, Miss," she began, aiming her words at the flight attendant and adopting a thick, clueless-sounding Southern accent from the United States. "I'm sure this handsome feller means well, but he's clearly confused. He *really* seems to think he knows me—"

"Clever girl," the man said, smiling at her shrewdly. "But you are operating on a false premise. One that will burn you in the end."

"I'm sure that I don't know what you mean," Lia said.

She smiled at him sweetly, her eyes as blank as a doll's, mostly for the stewardess's benefit. The man's eyes were what captured her, however.

A hard, near-flame rose behind those pale green irises.

Briefly, Lia held her breath, wondering if she'd made a mistake, if she'd pushed him too far. Something in his eyes gave her pause, even with the stewardess standing right there. As much as a perverse part of her was enjoying pushing his buttons, another, likely more sensible part of Lia wondered if she should just give him the ring.

Clearly, he was going to cause problems for her if she didn't.

Before she'd quite tipped over that threshold, the captain was walking up to them from the front of the plane. Since she was on an American airline, the man was American, and tall and white. When he spoke, Lia found herself thinking his Southern accent was likely real.

"Sir?" the captain said. "I'm going to need you to go to your seat. Now. Or we'll have to leave you here in Kathmandu. We can't have you bothering the plane's other passengers."

Lia watched the man with the green eyes as he seemed to assess the situation.

He looked at the male captain, then at the stewardess... then back at her, Lia.

He smiled only at Lia.

"Why, of course," he said, smiling even more widely at her. "I wouldn't wish to cause any sort of *scene.*" His grin widened more, turning shark-like. "The last thing on *Earth* I'd want is to delay the travels of these good, fine, upstanding citizens."

The stewardess exchanged looks with the captain, then sighed in obvious relief.

"Thank you, sir. We appreciate your cooperation."

The man with the leaf-green eyes never took them off Lia's face.

He continued to watch her as he let the stewardess steer him down the aisle, towards a seat located in the front part of the plane, which had to be first or business class.

The captain lingered by Lia for a moment.

"Are you okay, Miss?" he said.

She smiled her thousand-watt smile up at him.

"I'm great," she said, dropping the Southern accent for him, since he was actually a Southerner. "Thanks so much. I'm sure he's probably harmless but he was just so insistent he knew me. I admit, it was making me a little nervous."

"And you're absolutely, positively *certain* he had it wrong?" the man said, smiling at her teasingly. "You didn't know him, ma'am? Maybe you just forgot you disappointed him with a no, after he asked you out for dinner or a drink?"

Hearing the faint flirtation in his voice, she laughed, giving him her most charming smile.

"I'm pretty sure," she grinned, using an openly flirtatious voice.

"Maybe he just *wishes* he knew you, ma'am."

Lia grinned wider, looking over the tall, blond captain with the dark blue eyes.

"Maybe you do?" she said, quirking an eyebrow.

The captain flushed a little that time and laughed with her, right before he gave her a small wave and began to move off, following the stewardess and the man with the green eyes as he headed in the direction of the cockpit.

Maybe she could get off with him, she thought, watching the tall captain with the nice butt walking back towards the front of the plane.

That might keep green-eyes off her back, and it might discourage him from coming after her a second time. Like most men, he'd backed down pretty fast once he saw another male, and one in a position of authority.

If she walked off the plane with Captain Blue Eyes, her bizarre stalker might just leave her alone. Hopefully, he'd decide going after her was too much trouble, and write off the ring, or remember it was insured.

Then again, maybe he'd only played nice because the plane was still on the ground, and too close to the airport. Maybe he'd come after her again after the plane took off, and maybe he wouldn't care so much that time if he got threatened by airline employees.

Maybe her best bet would be to pretend to go for her connecting flight, and instead get off in Bangkok after she went through customs. She could simply "miss" the flight to L.A., hop a second flight to Chiang Mai, or Singapore, or Manila, or Kuala Lumpur.

Or she could disappear in Bangkok itself for a few days.

Lia knew people in Thailand.

She might even be able to unload the ring there, keep Fonzo's cut, and do the deal herself, face-to-face.

Thais liked gold.

They particularly liked old gold, gold with some symbolic or cultural meaning, even if it wasn't theirs. More to the point, Thais knew how to *sell* gold, especially to wealthy Chinese. Thousands of Chinese shopped in Thai markets and malls as they passed through Bangkok on their way to island vacations, or trips up north to ride elephants in Chiang Mai.

Thinking about this, frowning a little as she settled back into her seat, Lia decided she would get off in Thailand.

The sooner she unloaded this freak's stuff, the better.

3

THE ONE RING

L ia didn't take the Valerian root to sleep.

Or the Melatonin.

She figured, as disappointing and annoying as it was, with that nut following her onto the plane, she'd better keep her wits about her.

She had all three seats to herself, though, so it was a bummer.

She ended up with an old woman in the seat behind her, a family of Chinese people to the left of her, taking up the entire middle section of her row, and a South African couple in front of her.

After scoping out her immediate environment in full, making sure no one was paying any attention to her, Lia pulled her small laptop out of her leather satchel and signed into the plane's wifi.

Despite her decision to lose the weirdo in first class during her layover in Bangkok, Lia thought it couldn't hurt to get a second opinion on the ring. Pulling the object in question carefully out of a hidden pocket in her long, green leather coat, she discreetly took a photo of it with her laptop camera.

Disappearing the ring back into the hidden compartment in her jacket, she sent the photo to Fonzo, just to see if he had an opinion as to what it might be worth.

If he decided the ring was worth holding onto, or if he gave her valuable information on where it came from, she'd cut him in some, after she unloaded it in Bangkok.

Fonzo could be cool like that.

He was loyal to Gregor... bizarrely so, in Lia's mind... but Fonzo wasn't wholly adverse to helping her out on the side, fencing objects d'art and finding clients for deals that didn't necessarily have anything directly to do with the Syndicate or Gregor.

Anyway, Lia felt no guilt.

The ring was hers.

She'd done the job Gregor sent her to do in Nepal. He would get his stupid intel, as soon as she handed the flash drive over to Fonzo in L.A. Anything else she'd done while she was in Asia was none of Gregor or the Syndicate's damned business.

Fonzo would get that.

Despite his loyalty to Gregor, Fonzo was aware of, and sympathetic to Lia's situation.

He generally helped her out when he could, as long as it wasn't going directly against his bosses or Gregor, or might cause the Syndicate itself harm.

Besides, if the ring turned out to be worthless, maybe she'd give it back to the guy, just to get him off her ass. That would allow her to return to California, and, more importantly, keep Lia's new stalker from learning anything specific about her or who she worked for.

That would keep her out of hot water with Gregor, too.

Three waving dots showed up in the corner of her text screen a few minutes after she sent the photo and her query to Fonzo.

Then Fonzo's words popped up below hers.

I've seen this, he wrote. *Just this morning. I swear this exact ring was in one of the alerts that got sent around.*

Lia frowned, typing. *No shit? Seriously?*

Yep, he wrote. *Weird, right? I mean, what are the odds?*

You're sure it's this one? This exact ring?

Pretty sure. Looked a hell of a lot like this. You said you just lifted if off a guy in Nepal? What did he look like?

Lia wrote back, describing the green-eyed man as best she could, down to his black and gold tattoos, his open shirt and leather coat, the odd, horned, silver pendant he wore around his neck, the long black and red hair.

The way he'd followed her onto the plane.

He sounds handsome, chica, Fonzo wrote back teasingly. *Is he handsome? Did he follow you on the plane, looking for love? You got the hots for your crazy ring-bearer?*

Lia frowned, remembering that riveting gaze.

He's not ugly, she admitted in her next text. *He's... unusual-looking. Not someone who blends in. But his hotness isn't going to keep him from beating me up and taking the ring I stole, Fonzo. So maybe focus, okay?*

Her partner sent a string of laugh emojis.

Immediately afterwards, he began to type.

Okay. Let me look into it. I'm going to contact the buyer. Definitely don't give the ring to that guy, though, not until you hear back. If it's the merchandise in the alert, the price tag on this one is high. Do what you have to for now, but lose the hot weirdo with the freaky eyes if you can.

Lia glanced up and down the aisle, muttering, "Little tough on a plane, Fonzo."

She didn't write that part.

Instead she waited, looking between their dormant text window and the aisle of the plane, with occasional glances out the oval view port to the clouds and blue sky.

A few minutes after that, Fonzo wrote her again.

Definitely the same ring. I got the client to send me a few more photos and they're a definite match. You hit the jackpot, sweetie! I mean, what are the odds you'd pick up something like THAT in a random grab? In NEPAL of all places? The guy looking for it is based in San Francisco, and he sounds super motivated, chica. He's ready to fly to L.A., with money to spend. Can you bring it to me? Send me your flight number and I'll be there when you land.

Lia cursed under her breath.

If the price tag was as big as Fonzo was saying, there was no way she'd be able to keep Gregor out of this. He'd want his cut. She'd probably end up with less than if she sold it on her own in Bangkok.

Thinking, she wrote him back.

This jackass will probably follow me to Los Angeles, you know. He seems as obsessed with the ring as your guy in S.F.

There was a bare pause, then Fonzo wrote her again.

The buyer claims he knows him. Describes him pretty much exactly the way you did. If it makes you feel any better, sounds like your guy might have stolen it.

"Shocker," she muttered under her breath.

So her hot, weirdo, green-eyed ring-stalker was also a thief.

What the hell was it about this ring?

One stupid ring couldn't really be that valuable, could it?

She poked her head up from the laptop, glancing up and down the two aisles breaking up the different rows of seats.

The old Thai woman in the seat behind Lia was dead asleep.

The South African couple seated in front of her were

watching an action movie on a tablet. The Chinese family to Lia's left all appeared to be staring at their phones, with the exception of the father, who had his eyes closed, his head tilted back as he snored.

She hadn't seen the black and auburn-haired man since the stewardess led him away.

Somehow, *not* seeing him made her nervous.

She needed to go for a walk now that the seatbelt signs were off, figure out where the guy was sitting so she'd at least get some warning if he came at her a second time. She would have bet good money she hadn't seen anywhere near the last of him.

After another few minutes of thinking, she wrote to Fonzo.

You sure it's worth it? This guy seems a little nuts. I could dump it, try to get you and Gregor some better merchandise in Bangkok. I know a few art dealers there who might play ball. Expats in the import-export business. From what a few told me, rich locals are buying expensive pieces for vanity purposes and not guarding them for shit.

Fonzo wrote back almost at once.

We're talking half a million payday with your crazy-random pickpocket grab, chica. Bring that thing home. I already talked to Gregor. He's giving you three times your usual cut on this, since you went off the reservation.

Lia scowled, folding her arms.

The three dots rippled again, then Fonzo added,

Don't worry about the guy. My client says he's been looking for him. He definitely sounds confident he can handle him, and might even kick in a little extra for us bringing the thief to him. We'll have our own security there, too. Syndicate people.

Lia pursed her lips.

She was skeptical, but Fonzo was right.

It was a lot of money.

Bringing half-a-million in bonus cash to the boss was hella tough to turn down, especially now. A big payday like this might even be enough to get Gregor to let his sister go. Lia could try to use it to get herself out of the worst of her debt, argue to Gregor that she was making him more money than her mother ever lost for him.

If she could get her sister out of there, everything would be better.

Lia could even keep working for Gregor; if she knew Maia was safe, she might not even mind. She'd get the two of them a place, an apartment or even a house, maybe somewhere in the valley. Somewhere decent, with good schools.

If she squared things more with Gregor, she might even be able to start putting some money in the bank, set up a college fund for Maia.

Her sister would finally be safe.

She'd finally have a future.

More of a future than Lia likely had, thanks to dear ol' mom.

Thinking about that, imagining seeing her baby sister in the flesh for the first time in months, Lia decided she didn't give a crap about some dude with riveting green eyes and long black and auburn hair and a hot body, no matter how crazy he was, or how much intelligence she'd seen behind that smirk on his face.

She'd ditch him, just like Lia ditched any guy who made the mistake of assuming she was some blond idiot they could easily bully or manipulate.

That, or Fonzo's and Gregor's boys would make short work of him back in L.A.

Or that mysterious client, assuming he wasn't all talk.

Okay, she wrote her partner. *I'll catch my connecting flight to L.A. Just don't leave me hanging, F. There's something about this guy.*

He doesn't seem like the type to make empty threats. And he might be batshit, but he doesn't strike me as stupid, either.

We'll be there, chica. Just bring the ring.

Frowning a bit, Lia closed her laptop, again staring down the aisles of the plane in both directions. She stared longest in the direction the stewardess had taken the man with the long hair, and those stunning, armor-piercing green eyes.

Strangely, she felt almost bad about leading him into a trap.

On the other hand... not her problem.

Lia couldn't afford to feel guilty about the fate of strangers who threatened her life.

She had her own crap to deal with.

◌◌◌

T he pretty blond human who stole his ring didn't notice when Loki took the seat behind her.

Then again, why *would* she notice?

Loki waited for the stewardess to leave him alone, then shape-shifted into a harmless-looking old human lady, a local, so the blond would be even more likely to dismiss him.

He walked back, and eased into one of the empty seats behind her, making no noise so she wouldn't wonder why he was taking his seat twenty or so minutes into the flight.

When the blond finally looked back, noting his presence, Loki pretended to look out the window.

He didn't have to see the dismissal in her eyes to know it was there.

Loki watched the human female pull the ring out of her coat.

He was tempted to reach through the gap between the seats, take it from her right then and there, but curiosity stayed his hand, causing him to watch as she photographed it, using her small machine, then began speaking to someone with the keyboard.

He read over her shoulder, and she didn't notice that, either.

By the time she closed the laptop again, he even had the beginnings of a plan.

4

JUST A TASTE

Lia jumped violently when someone sat down in the
vacant aisle seat next to hers for a second time.
Instinctively, even before she turned her head to
look at who it was, she felt for the ring in her coat pocket and
glanced down at her feet, looking for her satchel and the top
of the pale pink laptop case poking out. Alarm ran through
her belly as she realized she'd dozed off, and she wasn't
entirely sure for how long.

Minutes, surely.

It couldn't have been more than minutes, could it?

Her internal clock told her it wasn't long.

All of that happened before she managed to refocus her
eyes on the strange woman now sitting in the seat next
to her.

Lia wasn't any less confused when she realized it was the
old woman who'd been seated directly behind her.

The woman, who still looked Thai to Lia, smiled at her
with thin lips and dark eyes, her round cheeks wrinkled and
strangely tanned below her halo of snow-white hair. She held
her hands out in front of her body strangely, her thin arms

poking out from the knitted wrap she wore. Something about the pose reminded Lia of a rabbit standing on its hind legs.

Lia was still blinking, trying to wake up, when the old woman raised one of those hands, giving her a little wave. Then the old woman simpered, giggling.

Lia blinked.

"I think you have the wrong seat," she said finally, pulling herself upright in her seat and combing her fingers through her long, blond hair. "Do you need help with something? Shall I call a stewardess for you?"

The old woman lowered the waving hand, staring at Lia for an uncomfortably long-feeling few seconds.

Then she spoke.

The voice that came out of her made Lia jump nearly a foot, pressing her back and body into the window and the curved bulkhead behind her.

"Were you dreaming about sex, my pretty?"

It was a man's voice.

Worse, it was familiar.

The little old Thai woman smirked.

After a pause, she spoke again, her voice still sounding *exactly* like that of the black and auburn-haired man whose ring Lia had in her pocket.

"It sure looked like you were," the old woman said. She quirked an eyebrow at Lia. "It sure smells like you were. I would love a little taste..."

Lia fought back a scream, staring at the old woman in the knit shawl and the lime-green polyester pants. Lia continued to watch, horror widening her eyes and opening her mouth as the old woman's dark brown eyes changed color, morphing into a pale green, growing so pale and translucent, they seemed to glow with an internal light.

"Come on, lover," the old woman cajoled.

Her face began to morph, the hair darkening, lengthening, transforming back into that black and auburn mane Lia remembered so clearly. Letting out a little yelp, she jerked back even further, drawing her legs up on the seat until she was half-crouched on top of it. She pressed her body as deep into the seat as she could cram herself, staring at him, wide-eyed, gripping the bulkhead just above the oval view port, fighting to breathe.

It was him.

Even the clothes had changed back to what she remembered from before.

Lia stared at him, then looked down at the call button on her armrest.

Before she could reach for it, the man leaned over swiftly. He placed a finger on the call button, grinning up at her from where he bent over the seat. There was a faint flash of light, a little *pop* sound, and the lit symbol of a woman in a triangle dress went dark.

Touching the call buttons on the other two armrests, he repeated the exercise.

After two more faint *pop* sounds, those went dark too.

The long, sinuous body of the man with the leaf-green eyes stretched out a hand and arm.

He caught hold of her wrist, tugging her easily back down beside him.

"Come now, my precious little elf," he said pleasantly. "Let us talk. Shall we?"

Lia reluctantly lowered herself back into the cloth seat, never taking her eyes off his face. She was breathing harder, but something in his expression eased the worst of her terror, making her more confused than fearful for her life, or even afraid that she might be losing her mind.

She stared at those pale, glowing, otherworldly eyes, trying to form words.

"Oh, no, you don't need to speak... not yet," the man soothed.

Before she could take another breath, he pushed up the armrest and slid half into her seat with her, pulling her leg around so that her back was to the view port, and he more or less positioned himself between her legs.

"They know about you," Lia blurted, staring at him. "I don't mean on the plane. I mean back home. In Los Angeles. If you take the ring now, it won't help you. There are people waiting for you—"

"Shhh, precious. I know... there, there."

The man with the green eyes smiled his wicked smile, studying her face openly. There was something inhuman about him, almost predatory, like a hawk staring down at something it might want to eat. Strangely, there was also something guileless in that look, like he wasn't hiding anything, including anything about his motives.

His hand, instead of going for the coat Lia was wearing, and the ring, slid into the V between her legs, pressing hard before he began massaging her in that spot, still watching her eyes.

"How about that taste now, my lovely elf?" he said, smiling wider. "I got ever so hungry, watching you dream about me... watching you imagine my cock massaging your cunt. What a dirty, naughty little thief you are..."

Lia swallowed, staring up at that face.

As she did, flickers of the dream she'd been having before the old woman sat down rose in the darkness behind her eyes.

She *had* been dreaming about him.

The dream had been so vivid, she even questioned whether she was really asleep.

Kind of like she was doing right now.

She'd been sitting here, with the light off, reading on her laptop, reading a book she'd been meaning to get to for weeks. She must have paused, rested her eyes. She doubted everything now, after watching him transform right in front of her.

Maybe she was sleeping still.

Maybe she was still dreaming about him.

"I see that mind of yours working, working, working... turning, turning, turning." Gauging her expression, her flushed cheeks, the uncertainty in her eyes, he grinned. "But you aren't asleep anymore, my lovely. And after watching you dream, I might have to give you what you asked for in that other space—"

She let out a shocked gasp, then a low moan when his hand slid inside her pants, his long fingers curling inside her.

She didn't really want him to stop, though.

She couldn't remember the last time she'd had sex. She couldn't even remember who it had been with, or whether she'd liked them much. This life, post mom running out of them, hadn't left a lot of time for anything Lia. It was all work, Gregor, worrying about her sister, worrying about getting caught, anger at her messed-up circumstances, anger that she'd lost any chance of a normal life, free of the debts her mother left.

Gregor would never let her go.

Never.

She grasped the man's arm, staring up at those leaf-green eyes, and he smiled at her, his fingers dexterous to the point where she could feel herself building, her heart pounding in her chest, so loud she was sure he could hear it.

"Ah, yes... my little kitten wanted to be pet. She *longed* to be pet, didn't you, lovely? Is that what makes you such a naughty little snack? Not enough stroking and petting and fucking in your world...? Not enough *you* in your world, perhaps?"

She let out a shocked groan, bucking against his fingers as

she came, and the green-eyed man leaned down, kissing her mouth as his other hand slid up her shirt.

He massaged her breasts, skillfully and roughly and sensually, making her back arch, her breath come in ragged pants. He found the clasp of her bra in front, somehow tugging it open with a single pull of his fingers. Yanking down her shirt, he lowered his mouth to her nipple, and then his fingers were stroking her again, and she was so slick she was whimpering with each pulling touch.

She came again, and that time, she pressed her mouth against his arm, if only to keep from crying out.

The man pulled up off her long enough to unbuckle the front of his pants.

He motioned towards her with graceful flicks of his fingers.

His green eyes shone hard now, filled with a dense desire that caught her breath in her throat, making her pant harder, until she could scarcely breathe.

"Take off your clothes," he said, his voice a hard command. "Now, elf. I'm going to fuck you until your cunt sucks on my cock…"

She didn't think.

She did as he said.

She forgot about the stewardesses, about the South African couple sitting in front of them, the Chinese family with their three kids on her other side. Something told her none of them would see anything, just like she'd seen an old Thai lady instead of this man when he sat down next to her for the second time.

She glanced past his shoulder, still fighting to breathe, looking at the family across the aisle. They were all staring at their phones still, the father snoring loudly with his head cushioned between a neck pillow and the edge of his wife's reclined seat.

"Now, elf," the man said, his voice thick. "Now. Or I'll be forced to punish you further."

She got her pants the rest of the way off and he yanked her hips down so that she lay beneath him on the three seats she'd gotten to herself. He inserted his body between her legs, coiling an arm dense with muscle under her knee and yanking up her leg so that it was nearly over her head.

He plunged his cock into her without waiting, all the way to the hilt.

Lia couldn't help it—she let out a low groan, loud enough that the entire cabin should have heard it.

No one turned their heads.

No stewardesses ran down the aisle to stop them.

He arched into her again, harder, and she was sweating now, holding his shoulders.

The strange pendant he wore, the chunk of silver with the curved horns, swayed back and forth over her, slapping into his gold and black tattooed chest with a soft thud. He closed his eyes, longer than a blink, and she saw longing fill his face, a pained want that made her reach for his face, then his hair, clenching her fingers in his long, shockingly soft locks.

He let out a heavy groan, and began fucking her harder, slamming her into the seat.

She came again... and again.

What the hell was he doing to her?

Was this a dream? This had to be a dream.

Someone would have stopped them.

She told herself it had to be a dream right up to the moment he finally climaxed, gripping her hips and altering her position with his hands and weight so he could angle into her as deeply as he possibly could. She felt him start to come inside her and groaned, so turned on she came again, with him.

He gripped her around her bare ass, forcing himself even deeper.

He was bucking against her then, coming a second time.

"Ah, yes," he groaned, his words nearly a purr. "Yes, we will be friends now, little one. I don't think I'm going to get tired of this for a long, long time."

Her legs wrapped around him as she continued to spasm, and the man over her seemed to glow as she looked up at him.

She'd never felt a cock so tangibly, every millimeter of its length, every curve and vein and soft stretch of skin, in her life. He was big as fuck, so that was part of it, but she swore the damned thing let off some kind of low electric charge inside her as well. She could feel his skin react to her spasms as her own anatomy fought to deal with his.

Even as she thought he might come again, he did, releasing into her, harder that time, so hard it made her groan even louder than she had before.

What. The. Ever-Living. Fuck.

He finally slowed his body.

He slowed it gradually as he let go, losing control in a way she could tangibly see. She watched his face grow soft, his jaw harden as he gasped, grinding into her.

A few more minutes must have gone by.

Hell, she had no idea how long it had been.

At some point he was looking down, studying her eyes, still spasming into her. His own eyes reflected a flicker of surprise, what might have been relief, but a depth of relief, of need, that kind of blew her away, even as she felt something similar burning inside herself.

She was still looking at that, studying it, trying to understand it—

When, out of nowhere—

That look on his face changed.

It changed into something she'd never seen, at least never aimed at her, Lia Winchester. She stared up at his face, feeling the emotion it conveyed as much as seeing it in his features, in those otherworldly eyes, in the determined set of his mouth.

It was like watching a life-changing decision unfold.

Maybe a kind of revelation.

The full-blown possessive, uncompromising ownership as he looked at her, as if marking her with those eyes, telling her there was no possible way this wasn't happening again...

It was difficult to even look at.

Lia couldn't look away, though.

She stared up at him, and as she did, he thrust into her even deeper, his cock still hard as steel, but the skin on it soft as velvet, touching every part of her.

"I'm afraid you might belong to me now, little elf," he said, staring into her, his cock seeming to go all the way through her. "...And I to you. I'm sure your current owners will find that problematic, so I'll just have to deal with them for you. Would you like that, little elf? Would you like me to own you, instead of the bad man who is mean to your sister?"

Staring up at that shockingly handsome face, the pale green eyes...

Lia had absolutely no idea what to say.

5

AIRPORT SHOPPING

If the stewardess thought it strange that Lia now shared her row with the man she'd requested be removed from that exact spot, a few hours earlier, no hint of it showed in her calm, perfectly made-up face.

She merely smiled at the two of them demurely when the drink and snack carts made their last circuit through the cabin, handing Lia's new friend a bourbon on the rocks, and giving her a cranberry juice and ice water.

When they landed in Bangkok, Lia followed the green-eyed man off the plane, still trying to pull her head and body back together, still fighting to convince herself she was actually awake, and not stuck inside some kind of twisted, super pervy dream with a complete stranger who initially threatened to kill her over a stolen ring.

At the same time, her mind was working again, moving chess pieces around the board, trying to make sense of what was happening now.

She assumed they wouldn't be going to Los Angeles.

Not anymore.

The green-eyed man made it crystal clear he'd seen all of

her back and forth texts with Fonzo, and knew exactly what
awaited them in LAX. She assumed they'd be catching a
different connecting flight, one to Moscow, perhaps, or
Rome, or maybe even the Philippines, so she was shocked
when he led her to a departure gate in Bangkok's Suvarnab-
humi International Airport and the marquee above the desk
read "TO: LOS ANGELES / LAX."

Lia came to a dead stop, staring up at the readout.

The man with her stopped as well, arching an eyebrow as
he looked at her.

She swore he was better-looking now than he had been
when she first laid eyes on him in Nepal. She saw women and
men staring at him with his open shirt, the strangely pirate-
like demeanor of him, those stunning eyes and full lips, his
high cheekbones and his long, thick hair, which hung and
curled perfectly down his back.

He seemed to notice her looking him over, and smirked.

"Are you liking me more now, little elf?" he said, caressing
her cheek with his fingers. "I'm sure we can find some privacy
in here somewhere, if you'd like me to fuck you again."

She felt her cheeks bloom with heat, especially when a
man standing nearby jumped, looking over at the two of them
before his eyes settled on Lia, his eyebrows rising inquisi-
tively as he glanced down her body, a faint smile on his lips.

Pushing aside the man's semi-suggestive stare, Lia focused
on the man with her.

"We're going to Los Angeles?" she said. "You know what's
waiting for us there."

"I do, yes," the green-eyed man said, smiling faintly.
"What is your name? Not that I mind calling you 'Little Elf,'
as it suits you so, but since I intend to keep you with me for
some time, perhaps even a good long while, assuming we can
come to some mutual arrangement, I would prefer something
formal to use as well, for when the occasion demands it."

"Lia," she said, blurting out her name before thinking about whether that was a good idea. "Lia Winchester."

"And who is this sister you think about so often, Lia Winchester? What is her name?"

Lia swallowed, staring at him. "How do you know I have a sister? How do you know anything about that? I never told you about her."

"And yet I do know. I know many things that have gone through your mind in the last few hours, Lia Winchester. What is her name?"

Lia felt her jaw harden.

She considered not answering, then realized that ship had sailed.

"Maia," she said, gruff.

She felt her eyes smart, and realized she was fighting off tears.

"Well, Lia Winchester," the man with the green eyes said, smiling at her. With surprising gentleness, he used his thumb to wipe a tear off her cheek. "You asked me if we are going back to Los Angeles. Well, the answer is yes. You implied a further question, which is *why* are we going there. Well, your darling sister is there, correct? And I assume we must fetch her, yes? We cannot simply *leave* her with that awful man?"

Lia stared at him, feeling her heart lurch sideways in her chest.

Whatever she'd expected him to say, it wasn't that.

"Maia?" she said, dumbfounded. "We're going back for Maia?"

The man smiled. "Do you not intend to ask me my name? Or must I listen to your bizarre recitation of my physical attributes in your mind for the next however-many hours, until you are *forced* to learn my name... perhaps by accident?"

She swallowed, blinking up at those stunning eyes.

Realizing he wasn't going to tell her, even now, unless she asked, she cleared her throat.

"What is your name?" she said.

"Loki," he replied at once. "I am Loki, God of Mischief. And you no longer belong that that man, 'Gregor,' or his 'Syndicate,' or whatever it is. You are mine now. Is that agreeable to you? I'm open to various sorts of negotiations. Be advised, I *will* withhold sex if you displease me, or refuse me one of my rather eccentric indulgences. Or if I catch you being overly friendly with one of the other humans wandering this world."

He waggled a finger at her.

"No random cock-sucking or fucking other humans, not without prior agreement. No kissing or fondling, either. I will throw an absolute tantrum. I'm petty like that."

Lia blinked again.

She honestly couldn't tell if he was pulling her leg.

Remembering the old Thai woman, and watching him transform in front of her, she went back to wondering if he'd dosed her with LSD, or possibly hypnotized her.

That, or maybe she was still curled up on that airplane seat, on her way between Kathmandu and Bangkok, and none of this was real.

"Really?" He quirked an eyebrow at her. "That is going to get quite old."

Watching her for a moment or so longer with his narrowed, leaf-green eyes, he sighed a little, tugging affectionately on a lock of her long, blond hair.

"Okay, little elf," he told her. "You may think about it a while longer. I would like an answer before we arrive in Los Angeles, however."

He checked the clock on the wall, motioning her towards one of the duty-free stores in the airport causeway. His fingers flickered specifically and gracefully towards one that sold women's clothing.

"In the meantime, I can feel you want to fuck more. I do, as well. We have an hour to kill. I want to get you into clothes that provide me a lot more access. I don't mind sending up mirages so no one can see what we're doing... but bras confound and irritate me, and I want to be able to finger your cunt whenever the mood strikes me."

Lia felt her whole body react to his words, even as she winced, looking away from his eyes, glancing at the store where he'd motioned with a hand.

"I'll purchase it," he said, winking at her with a smirk. "But only if I get to pick it out. Like I said, I have *very specific requirements,* little elf. Requirements I hope you'll be amenable to. I plan to fuck you a lot during this little journey. I want you completely addicted to my cock and come by the time we arrive back in your home town, and you're forced to make a final decision about me."

Loki paused, giving her a short bow.

"As a matter of full disclosure, I do not blackmail those I am courting, however... or those with whom I would like to be intimate. Therefore, the offer to save your sister stands, regardless of your decision."

Lia swallowed, but followed him willingly enough when he offered her his arm.

Sliding her hand and forearm through the crook in his elbow, she let him lead her into the clothing store, and over to the manikins in the back that wore summer dresses, suitable for Bangkok's hot and humid weather, and relatively suitable for Los Angeles in the summer.

She watched "Loki" as he wandered among the displays, his lips pursed as he assessed each article of clothing.

Occasionally, he glanced back at her, looking her up and

down critically, as if trying to imagine what the dress or skirt might look like on her.

She knew when she saw his eyes light up that he'd found something he liked.

"Come here, little elf."

He beckoned her closer, and she saw him standing in front of a short, white, micromini dress made of thin fabric. It had a halter top with a plunging neckline and looked like it would barely cover her crotch.

"You have nice, big, fat tits," he informed her, grinning. "I want to see you in this. Your nipples should strain right up against that material, giving me a nonstop hard-on. We're definitely trying this on."

He eyeballed her again, then grabbed one of the dresses off the rack, choosing a size smaller than Lia would have chosen for herself for the same dress.

Taking her hand, he led her to the dressing room, walking her past the confused salesperson and into one of the try-on booths.

Pulling the curtain closed, he hung up the dress, then walked up to her, grabbing hold of her leather coat and pulling it off her arms and shoulders.

He hung that on a different hook, then stared at her black jeans and the T-shirt she wore.

"Okay," he said, motioning up and down with a finger. "Take it off. All of it."

Lia only hesitated a second, then grabbed the bottom of her white T-shirt and yanked it up over her head. She laid her hands on the leather belt she wore, but Loki shook his head, walking closer.

"No, no... the bra first. I want to look at those glorious tits while you finish undressing."

Flushing, she reached up, undoing the front clasp and shouldering off her bra, watching his eyes in spite of herself, seeing the heat that rose there when she first freed her breasts.

He stared at her for a few seconds while she stood there, arms at her sides. His throat moved in a swallow. He motioned towards her again.

"All right," he murmured, his voice thicker. "Now the belt and pants."

She unhooked the leather belt, then began pushing the jeans off her hips and down her legs. He watched her step out of the last of them, then he motioned towards her again.

"All of it, little elf."

She felt herself flush hotter as she removed her underwear.

When she looked up, he was smiling at her again, that heat even more prominent in his eyes. "I do appreciate how accommodating you are, little elf. I might have to buy you more presents before we leave here." Smiling at her more warmly, he motioned towards the dress hanging on the hook to her right. "Put it on."

Pulling the dress off the rack, she was even more struck by how thin the material was. There was no possible way it wasn't see-through, especially if the light hit it right. Regardless, she pulled it over her head, adjusting it around her upper body and waist until the bottom part fell down over the rest of her torso.

He'd been right. Her breasts strained against the thin material in the size he'd gotten for her, making her nipples instantly hard.

He walked up to her, caressing one with a hand, making it harder still.

Every part of her ached for him now.

Her breath shortened as she watched him look at her. When he reached up with his other hand, massaging her second breast, she let out a soft moan, cutting it off by biting her lip. Her eyes never left his, or the heated stare he aimed down the rest of her.

"Very nice," he said approvingly, cupping and squeezing her breasts. "I want to fuck you right now, little elf, but I think I'm enjoying watching you squirm a little too much to give you what you want just yet."

Sitting down on the bench in the dressing room, he unhooked his belt, unfastening the front of his pants and freeing his cock.

It was even bigger than it felt when he'd had it inside her.

She stared at him, feeling him watch her look.

"You're going to kiss my cock now, little elf. Oh, and you're *not* going to come. You're going to suck and kiss me until I come, and swallow every drop, but if *you* come, I'll know it, and I'll punish you horribly, unspeakably, for the entire flight. You won't have a single orgasm, and I'll make you watch me fuck other humans in front of you. Even if you try to suck off other male passengers, *they* won't be allowed to make you come, either... do you understand? Are you hearing me, little elf?"

"Yes." Her voice came out husky, almost strangled.

"Now come here," he said. "Kneel down and suck me like I can feel you want to. I want your knees spread, your tits pushed up, your back arched. I want to watch you suck me and wish the whole time it was your cunt and not your mouth."

Lia found herself kneeling in front of him, her hands splayed on his thighs as she kissed the head of his cock, then ran her tongue down the length of him. She took him in her mouth next, and Loki sucked in a hissing breath.

He let her do that a few more times without moving. He sat there, leaned back against the wall of the dressing room, muscles clenched.

Then he was pulling her hair out of the braid she'd tied it

in, unwinding the strands and burying his hands in her blond locks. Gripping her tightly in both hands, he groaned louder, right before he began thrusting his cock deeper into her mouth.

She controlled him, holding him back, teasing him with her lips, tongue and teeth.

He was building within seconds.

Lia couldn't remember any point in her life when she'd ever been so turned on, just from doing this. She was fighting to breathe, stroking him with one hand as her other hand and fingers explored as much of him as his clothes permitted. She took him all the way into her mouth and throat, and he groaned again, right before he began to let go.

He cried out as he climaxed.

She felt a kind of pleading, longing, disbelief in his cries, even as he gripped her tighter, groaning as he came into her mouth.

After he finished, he leaned back against the wall, watching her as she raised her head, wiping her mouth.

He beckoned to her again.

"Come here, little elf," he said, his voice a low murmur.

She sat up, then stood slowly, looking down at him.

"Spread your legs," he said. "Sit astride me. I want to feel how wet you are."

Another ripple of arousal went through her, even as she obeyed.

Spreading her legs, she slid onto his lap, and the dress rode up to cling to the edges of her ass. He slid a hand between her thighs, caressing her skin gently before inserting a single finger into her. He added another finger a few seconds later... then another.

He stroked her sensually, his eyes closed, caressing her inner thigh with his other hand from behind.

"Oh, that's nice," he murmured, his eyes still closed.

"You've got juice running down your legs, little one. I think I might have to decorate you with more of that before we arrive in Los Angeles."

Still flushing all over, and now biting her lip to keep from asking him for sex, she slid off his lap reluctantly when he pushed gently on her hips.

"We'd better go," he said, winking at her. "I have those other presents I must attend to, and I suspect it would be far too easy to miss our flight as it is."

She leaned down to pick up her underwear and her bra. She started to step into the underwear first to pull it up under the dress, but Loki, stopped her, shaking his finger and his head at her.

"No, no, no, my little elf. You weren't listening. I insist on full access. At all times. You will leave the underwear here."

She stared at him.

Looking at herself in the mirror with the dress, it barely seemed to cover her. The hem hung down only an inch or two to cover the tops of her thighs. Her nipples pressed up against the thin material and the tight fabric outlined every part of her breasts.

If she reached up, or bent down, the fabric would ride up and she'd more or less flash her ass and privates to the whole world.

She started to stuff the underwear in her satchel, thinking she might be able to put it on later, at least, when they arrived in Los Angeles, but Loki took them from her hand, and threw them over the wall of the dressing room.

Staring at the wall between the two dressing stalls, Lia bit her lip. She looked at Loki, taking in that lazy half-smile, seeing the heat in his eyes as he waited to see if she would go after them, or yell at him, or simply insist on wearing something besides that liquid-thin dress.

As if hearing her thoughts, Loki shrugged.

"You can go get them, of course," he said mildly. "You can buy ten more pairs if you wish, my love. You can put on your jeans. You can wrap the coat around yourself. You can wear or do anything you wish. But I can't promise there won't be repercussions, my sweet, hot, wet little elf... so it really depends on how badly you want my cock on the flight to L.A."

Lia felt a shiver of heat run through her as she remembered the list of things he'd threatened her with once they got on the plane. The idea of watching him have sex with someone else, right in front of her, brought a dense pool of anger to her gut.

At the same time, the idea of giving some random guy head, some total stranger on the plane, just to please him, maybe even to make him jealous, made her thighs squeeze together, even as she averted her gaze from his.

Jesus, Lia, she scolded inside her head. *Get a grip on yourself. You're acting like this guy's personal sex slave.*

Loki let out a delighted laugh.

"Oh, I hope so, lover," he said to her fondly, leaning down to kiss her temple as he squeezed her ass through the thin material of the dress. "I can't tell you how much I hope that's what you want... because I will treat you so very, *very* well, if you do."

Lia swallowed, staring at those catlike green eyes, even as Loki reached out with his other hand, tracing her nipple through the thin, white material.

Her back arched involuntarily, and his smile widened, right before he kissed her mouth.

He lingered there, still tugging at her nipple as he ran his tongue lightly over her lips.

He breathed her in, tasting her tongue, and she shivered.

Taking his hand, she tried to bring it down between her legs, but he waggled his finger at her teasingly, grinning as he pulled at her nipple, making the skin crinkle and harden painfully.

She could feel the part of herself responding to everything he did, everything he said to her, even as she told herself she was just going along with this to get her sister free, to deal with the thing with Gregor, to keep herself safe from Loki himself.

Strangely, even in thinking it, she knew it was a lie.

As pushy and odd and bizarrely blunt Loki was, she didn't feel afraid of him.

Something about even his pushiness struck her as strangely hands-off.

Almost like a question lived behind every line he crossed.

Honestly, maybe she was crazy for thinking so, but she one hundred percent believed that Loki would leave her alone entirely if she asked. He might fuck someone else in front of her, like he'd threatened, but he wouldn't touch her if she told him no.

She didn't want to tell him no, though.

She couldn't explain that to herself, either, and honestly, she wasn't sure if she wanted to try. She wanted to get Maia away from Gregor. Maybe Loki could help with that, like he said, or maybe it was all just a scam to do with sex and the ring and whatever waited for them on the other side of the ocean.

She had a few more hours to think about that.

She had a few more hours with Loki before she had to come to any sort of conclusion, much less make any kind of decision.

She was more than willing to spend that time playing this particular game.

In fact, the idea of those hours of flight stretched out before them, given how Loki said he intended to pass the time, already had her breathing in short pants, even as she tried to hide it from those intense green eyes staring at her.

She bent down to pick up her bra—

Loki took that out of hand, too.

Instead of throwing it over the wall, he tossed it down on the bench behind him, watching her eyes, his eyebrow quirked in a silent question as he massaged her breast, as he waited to see if she would grab it, or try to cover herself again.

When she only stuffed her jeans, belt and T-shirt into her satchel, and picked up her leather coat, folding it over her arm, Loki smiled.

Seconds later, she walked out of the dressing room with him, her satchel slung over her shoulder, Loki's arm coiled possessively around her waist.

6

CHANGELING

He'd somehow arranged for them to have their own row again, even though the flight between Bangkok and Los Angeles was more or less full.

Before they'd even gotten on the plane, he'd had his hand under her dress more often than not. He'd pulled the dress up in the middle of a store to insert a small, metal vibrator inside her, turning it on and insisting she hold it there without coming or he'd spank her in the middle of the airport.

He said he might even do it without using what he called a "glamour" to keep others from seeing him do it.

The vibrator was one of the "gifts" he'd mentioned in the dressing room.

Others included nipple clamps, several types of lubricant, a blindfold, scarves to use on her wrists, a larger vibrator, and a collar.

While they were at the desk getting new boarding passes, he fingered her in front of the airline steward, talking to the man standing behind the counter in a cheerful voice while he pulsed the small metal vibrator deeper inside her, gripping and massaged her breasts and her ass with his other hand.

When she came abruptly against the ticketing counter, unable to stop it, Loki grinned at her wickedly, then informed her she would have to be spanked before they boarded the plane.

Unlike what he'd threatened, he must have kept the "glamour" in place, however, since no one so much as looked at them when he spread her over his lap and yanked up her dress. He spanked her until her ass cheeks stung, until she was panting, nearly coming again.

All the while, her face hung halfway in the lap of the guy sitting next to them in the boarding area, who was reading on his tablet and drinking a gourmet coffee.

She noticed the guy shifting uncomfortably in his seat.

Loki noticed too, and laughed, telling her that "the human" was responding to his "little nympho fuck-toy," even if the man couldn't see her.

When Loki noticed the man sported a hard-on that strained his gray suit pants, he informed Lia that the erection was her fault, and that she really should address it.

Lia got down in front of the guy, unfastening the pants.

She stroked him off, embarrassed at first, then getting increasingly turned on when the man responded, all the while Loki looked on, his hand gripping her hair as he kissed her mouth, sucking on her tongue while her hand massaged the man's cock.

The man blushed uncontrollably the whole time, looking around nervously every few seconds as he bucked gently against her palm, trying in vain to hide his arousal and then his orgasm behind his computer tablet as she finished him off.

She wondered what he told himself was happening.

She had a flush of guilt then, wondering if he was married or had a girlfriend—or a boyfriend—or if she'd just molested a total stranger regardless, and Loki laughed again.

"No, sweetness. Even the gods have to answer to karma. I know you won't believe me, but I asked him, and he gave me an enthusiastic yes."

Strangely, that made Lia feel a lot better about the whole thing.

Even more strangely, she *did* believe him.

She didn't believe Loki to be trustworthy, exactly, but she also never got the impression he was lying to *her*. She fully believed him capable of lying when it suited him, even creating elaborate storylines to deceive entire groups of people, if he could justify it according to his own twisted moral code and if it aided him in achieving his ultimate goals... but somehow, *this* didn't strike her as an area where he was deceptive.

If anything, Loki was brutally honest in this, and everything *this*-related.

She tried to decide if her conclusions in that regard were wishful thinking.

They didn't *feel* like wishful-thinking.

Lia usually had a really good radar when it came to whether she could believe someone. It was one of the things that made her a good thief. Her mom had called it "uncanny" when Lia was a kid, and even Maia called her "spooky" at times.

Also, Lia trusted her gut on this because she would have welcomed any excuse to dismiss everything about Loki as a depraved, immoral, reckless, disrespectful, and untrustworthy. She would have loved any excuse to convince herself he was a liar, a snake, a manipulator, someone who lacked any redeeming value as either a sexual partner or a human being.

She didn't really believe that, though.

Some part of Lia *wanted* to believe that, but she couldn't quite convince herself, and not only because just about everything about him turned her on.

As for Loki himself, that whole scene in the boarding area only seemed to jack him up even more.

They boarded the plane not long after, and before the flight had even taken off, he'd pulled her into his lap. After teasing her with his fingers and tongue, sucking on her breasts and fingering her until the plane was in the air, he finally gave her what she wanted and fucked her thoroughly, after removing the small vibrator and putting it in his pocket.

He ordered them drinks after they had sex the first time, with her still lying on her back, half-naked and sweating, writhing on the plane seats, fighting to catch her breath... then he turned her over and entered her from behind, yanking down the dress in front so he could fondle her breasts and tug on her nipples while he thrust languidly into her.

Of course, none of the other passengers saw it.

Still, something about *Lia* seeing all of those people there both mortified her and turned her on. Loki clearly felt that, because he brought her closer to other male passengers the next few times, fucking her right against one of them after pressing her into the man's lap, so that the man's erection pressed against her ass while Loki entered her from the front.

When he brought her back to their seats, he insisted she kneel in the space below him, where he fed her from his plate and stroked her hair.

He informed her that whenever his cock got hard—which was often—that it was her fault, and her responsibility to take care of.

He came on her breasts, and refused to let her wipe them off.

He came inside her... multiple times... enough to make her ask him about protection, about pregnancy and diseases... only to have him laugh and inform her he was a "god" and didn't get diseases, and that he could only impregnate her if he specifically *willed* a pregnancy into her.

He said he'd only do that if she asked nicely.

When she let him have his way in just about everything, he got even more turned on, until he laid her out on both seats again, taking his time while he drove into her for what felt like hours, bringing her to the brink only to ease her off, doing it again and again until she was whimpering and begging him.

He came inside her for a long time when he finally finished... so long, she found herself spasming against him, turned on to the point where she called out his name, wrapping her legs around his waist.

She had no idea she could get so turned on by another person.

She had no idea she could be sore from sex, and still want more, still crave more, to the point of sitting on his lap and thrusting her breasts in his face, asking him for it.

She'd never behaved like this in her life.

She began to wonder if he'd actually drugged her... if she was on some kind of insane, experimental aphrodisiac that turned her into an honest-to-gods nymphomaniac.

When he started fondling her again, stroking her insides with his fingers while he pinched and pulled at the clamps he put on her nipples, spreading her legs to get her to drip on his cock, she felt like she would have done almost anything he asked, *maybe* short of murder, if it meant he would bring her to another orgasm with his cock inside her.

Her whole body ached for him, for that magnificent cock, his dexterous fingers, his soft mouth, that freakishly sensitive tongue.

When she finally managed to doze off, about three-fourths of the way through the flight, when most of the cabin was sleeping and they'd lowered the lights, closing the shades over all the view ports, Loki woke her up an hour later with his tongue inside her again.

Again, he spent what felt like an hour on her, giving her head, kneading and massaging and stroking her all over, torturing her with his tongue and lips and teeth, until finally he raised himself up and thrust an enormous erection inside her, all the way to the root.

She nearly came right then.

She let out a weak moan as her cunt practically pulled him inside of her, and she groaned louder, clutching at him and begging him as he fucked her slowly, excruciatingly slowly, to an orgasm that nearly made her black out.

Instead of satisfying her, it just made that ache in her throb more.

She found herself whimpering in his ear, tugging on him before she turned around, bending over and thrusting her ass in his face.

He took her again, harder that time, and when he came, he yelled out her name.

He didn't call her "little elf" that time.

He called out her actual name.

His voice came out deep, guttural, with a power that made her buck against him.

He gripped her shoulder tightly in one hand, grinding and slamming into her as he lost control, his jaw clenched, growling with each thrust.

Something about that seemed to shift something between them.

She caught him staring at her after that, a dense probing in his eyes, mixed with a harder, hotter, more intense look that was difficult to look at without flushing and turning away.

He stared at her like that for a few minutes.

She told herself it meant nothing.

He continued to study her face until she was massaging the top of his chest, exploring his muscles, skin and bones with her fingers, tracing his gold and black tattoos, noting where his shirt stuck to him with sweat.

When he spoke, his voice was as deadly serious as his eyes.

"Don't play with me, Lia Winchester," he said.

She looked up, blinking at him in surprise. "Me?" She smiled. "I thought *we* were playing, Loki, God of Mischief. I thought that was the whole point."

He was already shaking his head.

His voice grew almost stern.

"If you don't intend to stay with me, if you plan to break and run as soon as I've finished delivering your sister to you, or as soon as I've freed you from this lecherous 'Gregor' and retrieved my ring... you'd better tell me now. If you don't, I will be most vexed. Most, most vexed. I will feel quite bothered, you see."

He paused, still staring at her eyes.

He seemed to be expecting an answer.

When she didn't give one, his green eyes darkened.

"I might be more than vexed," he added.

She blinked at him a second time, then half-smiled, thinking he must be teasing her.

This couldn't possibly be anything to him.

They'd barely spoken. He knew nothing about her.

He knew nothing about her life.

She knew nothing about his.

This simply was what it was: a freaky, perverted, sexual free-for-all between two relative strangers who had literally nothing else in common.

"That's not entirely true," he murmured, caressing the blond hair out of her face, leaning up to kiss her cheek.

"The ring?" she said, lifting an eyebrow and wrapping her

arms around his neck. "I figured you must've taken that from me by now."

"Not yet, my precious." He drew a line along her jaw with one finger. "And that is not what I meant."

"Then what did you mean?" she said, her voice still teasing.

He pushed her back slightly, giving her a harder look.

"I mean, *you and I,* little elf... and what you seem intent on refusing to see. We may be human and god, but we are far more alike than you seem willing to acknowledge. I would like to propose a partnership. I am realizing I could use help, now that my brother is *bound and determined* to stake out Earth and prevent me from enjoying this world."

She let out a short laugh.

"Your brother?" She snorted. "Which brother is that? Thor, God of Thunder?"

He gave her a level stare.

"You've got to be kidding—" she began.

"And yet I am not," he cut in. "You must learn to distinguish the difference with me, Lia Winchester. If we are to make this partnership work."

She stared at him, feeling a flicker of unease when she realized she almost believed him.

At any rate, he believed it.

His eyes told her Loki was dead serious.

"A partnership?" She leaned back, removing her arms most of the way off his neck. "I assumed once you got your ring back, and amused yourself breaking out Maia or whatever... that I'd never see you again."

"And yet I am telling you, and have told you repeatedly now, that I could use your help."

"How?" She frowned, feeling some of the sex haze starting to dissipate. "If you are who you say you are... which I'm not saying I believe *remotely,* by the way... what possible help could I be to you?"

"Do you have any idea how long it's been since someone has successfully pick-pocketed me, little elf? Do you have any idea how long it's been since *anyone,* human or god, has given me the slip?"

She frowned. "How long?"

"Never," he said, his voice hardening. "Never. Not my brother... not even my father. Not even the *real* elves, though they have certainly tried their share of pranks."

Lia continued to frown at him, not hiding her skepticism.

He wasn't exactly letting off alarm bells in terms of lying this time, either, but every word he said made no sense to her logical mind.

"You see?" he declared, aiming a finger at her. "That! That is what I am talking about! You *know* when I am lying. You *know* when I am telling the truth. Even when your logical mind tells you otherwise, you still *know.* You have instincts I don't fully understand, Lia Winchester, along with a skill set I can undoubtedly put to good use."

Still studying her eyes, his green ones narrowed when he added,

"You don't seem to have yet realized something about me, Lia dearest. If you had been the vast majority of humans, I would have taken the ring off you within *seconds* of catching up to you on that plane. I may still have defiled you... you are quite a tempting little plum, and I would have done it just for sport. But I would have left *immediately* after expelling my seed. I would have perhaps humiliated you a bit in the process for the thievery, perhaps leaving you without clothes when I lifted the glamour, but I likely would have exited the plane before it got off the ground in Kathmandu."

Loki's jaw hardened as he watched her think about this.

"I certainly wouldn't be *traveling to Los Angeles* with you," he went on, his voice a touch harder. "I would not risk encountering my brother. I would not risk exposing myself further by rescuing your sister. Certainly not to help someone who *stole* from me—"

She waved him off, frowning.

"So what are you saying?" she said. "You want to hire me? Is there some job you need done? Will I owe you for getting Maia away from Gregor?"

He stared at her, and she swore she saw bewilderment in his eyes that time.

"Because I'll do it," Lia added, still watching those pale irises. "Of course I'll do it. I'll help you out any way you want. If you get my sister out of there, and get us both away clean from Gregor, so she can have an actual *life*... free of those bastards... I'll help you pull whatever jobs you want. Even against 'Thor the Thunder God.'"

Lia smirked a little at that last; she couldn't help it.

Loki blinked, looking away as he seemed to think about her words.

Then he looked up at her, aiming that harder scrutiny at her face.

"Deal," he said, holding out a hand. "That is how you humans decide such things. Correct? You make 'deals' once you have agreed upon a basic set of arrangements between one another?"

"How do gods do it?" she said, hiding another smile.

"It is similar." Loki's eyes remained serious as they met hers. "Only I believe I can actually trust your word more, Lia Winchester. I think you would suck my cock every day until the day you died, if it would save your sister."

She snorted at that, rolling her eyes.

Even so, she felt a flicker of bewilderment, what verged on unease.

How did he know so much about her?

Why was he suddenly playing things so serious with her, after everything he'd done at the airport and on both planes? She continued to watch him, studying his eyes, sure he must be messing with her, even though her internal radar failed to give off a warning ping.

Despite the intensity she sensed below, Loki appeared almost calm now.

Even more strangely perhaps, despite all his previous smiling and winking, his eyes grew clear, containing a seriousness that verged on outright sincerity.

Loki now looked at her with a disarming openness, as if waiting for her reaction to him as this—someone able to be transparent—versus the vaguely threatening, openly smirky, deeply perverted, and unapologetically crass Loki of before.

She smiled wider, nudging him with her arms.

He didn't smile back.

He continued to look at her, that unnerving openness reflected in his light-filled eyes.

7

DISEMBARKING

"No, no, darling girl. Let them pass."

Lia lowered herself back to her seat, looking over at him.

Loki continued to watch people walk by, scanning face after face as he motioned with his jaw towards the back of the plane, giving her a sideways glance.

"We go out a different way, my precious," he told her.

She still wore the semi-indecent dress.

She still had no underwear on.

Unlike before, however, her long, dyed-green leather coat was wrapped around her shoulders, and it covered most of her, halfway down her calves to her bare feet. Loki told her to leave off on putting on her boots, at least until they were off the airplane. His instructions puzzled her, especially after she asked him why.

Loki had given her a faint smile, his eyes shrewd as he looked her over. "I'd prefer not to be kicked in the head with one or both of your boots, love... if it's all the same to you."

When Lia frowned, opening her mouth to ask him what the hell *that* meant, Loki held a finger to his lips, eyes warning as he continued to watch the other passengers collect their belongings and ready to leave the plane.

Sighing a bit, Lia let it go.

She also didn't put on her boots.

She stuffed them in her satchel instead, along with her T-shirt, jeans, socks, and laptop, which Loki also insisted on carrying for some reason. Her satchel also held the data stick with the intel she'd pulled for Gregor at the embassy building in Kathmandu, her change of clothes from traveling, a gold figurine she lifted from the market, various watches, wallets, rings, and necklaces she'd pickpocketed before she'd encountered Loki, and her own passport, California driver's license, and wallet.

It felt strange to hand all that over to him, but some part of her did it without question, without anything other than a purely-habitual flicker of unease. She watched him throw the strap over his neck and shoulder, the leather satchel bulging at his side, while Lia herself sat there with no shoes, the thin dress, and only the long leather coat to really cover her.

She associated the satchel so much with being a thief.

For the same reason, just handing it to him bonded her to Loki in a way more intimate than sex, connecting them on a deeper level, one she couldn't fully explain to herself.

Following Loki's eyes, copying his silent watchfulness, Lia sat next to him in their assigned seats as the rest of the passengers filed off the plane in the direction of the cockpit.

All of them looked like they were relieved to be on the ground again.

Faces flushed, skin dented in places from seat cushions, pillows, and rumpled blankets, they appeared bleary-eyed and mostly half-asleep. They lugged suitcases, backpacks, purses, small children, bags of souvenirs, even a little dog in a cloth case.

Loki was dressed again.

Lia still found him distracting as he propped his boot on the back of the chair in front of him, his shirt open at the top along with his leather coat, still somehow looking like a pirate with his long hair and the silver pendant around his neck, and the silver rings.

They sat there, more or less silent, until everyone had left the plane.

Then Loki nudged her, indicating that she should walk towards the airplane's tail.

"I've glamoured us," he commented. "They won't see us. But try not to walk into any flight attendants as we walk by, pet. It tends to confuse the illusion a bit."

"Why can't you just make us look like someone else?" she murmured, leaning towards his ear. "To get off the plane, I mean. Why not just make us look like old Thai women? Or stewardesses? Or the pilots?"

Loki smiled at her, winking as he continued to make his way down the aisle.

Both of them paused, inserting themselves into seat rows to let two airline attendants pass by on their way towards the front of the plane.

"Clever girl," Loki said next. "I'm glad to see you are catching on to my bag of tricks. Sadly, however, glamours do not work on my brother. He will see right through them. He may not recognize *you,* my darling, but he certainly will know *me.* That would be true no matter what form I took. Even in a crowd like this, he would pick me out easily."

Loki scowled as he said it, as if he resented the idea.

Really, more as if the whole notion of his brother recognizing him so easily offended him at a soul-level.

"Why does your brother want you, anyway?" Lia said.

She spoke quietly, glancing around them.

She knew it might not be necessary with the glamour, but

it was hard to remember that the people she could see and hear couldn't see or hear *her*.

"All for some ring?" she added, walking fast to keep up with Loki's longer strides. "What's the deal with that ring anyway? Why is it so important to you?"

"It is complicated, dearest girl, but suffice it to say: it's a magical artifact, I stole it, and my brother wants it back."

"So why not just give it to him?" She frowned, loping a bit faster to stay directly behind him. "Is it really worth all this trouble?"

"It might be." He glanced back at her, arching one of his dark eyebrows. "I did go to a fair amount of trouble to steal it. One might assume I had a reason for that, apart from annoying my brother... as fun as that can be."

"But you won't tell me what the reason is?" she persisted.

He sighed, as if her questions were exhausting him.

Or perhaps because he realized it would be easier to just tell her the truth.

In any case, in the end, that's what he did.

"I'm a bit concerned you might take this the wrong way," he said, giving her another over-the-shoulder glance. "But I felt compelled to take it, so that I could take over your world. More accurately, perhaps, I wish to wrest control of your world away from my father, who I believe is mismanaging it terribly."

Lia frowned, following behind him silently for a few seconds.

Then she burst out in an involuntary laugh.

"Did you just say you need the ring to conquer Earth? As in *my* Earth?"

Loki gave her a faint smile, shrugging.

"That's how my brother would term it, certainly. I see it rather differently. Well. It is semantics, perhaps. But I think my brother would misrepresent my intentions and methods wildly. He has a tendency to be a bit hysterical—"

"This is *Thor* we're talking, right?" she said, smiling in spite of herself. "Thor, the God of Thunder. *He's* the hysterical one?"

"This surprises you? I mean, come on. His gift is thunder and lightning. Loud noises. Big, crashing lights. Of course he's going to be a drama queen."

Lia burst out in another laugh, unable to help herself, and Loki glanced back at her with a genuine-looking smile.

"You are quite adorable when you laugh," he remarked, reaching behind him to catch hold of her hand, squeezing it in his. "I may have to ravish you again, when we get somewhere that isn't likely to end in one or both of us being caught and dismembered... or, sadly more likely in my case... sent to a cell beneath the palace grounds on Asgard."

Loki led her all the way to the rear of the plane, looking past the curtain to make sure no more cabin crew remained on that part of the aircraft. Lia could already hear the cleaning crew and maintenance team going through the cabin from the front end of the plane, likely to get it stocked and ready for the next flight.

"Come on, elf," Loki said, beckoning for her to join him behind the curtain.

Lia jerked her head and eyes back towards him, then followed him into the small galley area at the rear of the plane.

Once she was inside, he yanked the curtain closed behind her.

She watched him walk over to the rear, oval, exit door.

Loki examined the door's locking mechanism for a total of two seconds, then grabbed hold of the lever and threw it down, swinging the door outwards to smack against the outside the plane.

Lia watched, gaping, as he immediately stepped out of the tail end of the plane.

He disappeared from view, falling straight down with her satchel gripped tightly in one muscular hand, and Lia ran for the opening. Reaching it, she gripped the metal edges of the oval doorway, poking her head out to peer down at him.

Loki stood directly under the door, gazing up at her.

From the look of him, he'd landed easily on his feet.

He still gripped her satchel in one hand, at his right hip.

"God," she muttered under her breath. "He's a *god*, Lia. He can mesmerize people. Apparently he can also jump thirty feet and land like a cat…"

She watched Loki glance around the tarmac where he'd landed, still directly below the opening in the tail of the plane. A few seconds later, he looked up at her again. When she only stood there, he let go of her satchel at his hip.

He held up his hands and arms, beckoning with his fingers.

"Come, little one," he called up. "I think I've found us a route to the street, but we should hurry. There's some chance my brother could try to intercept us out here."

"I'm not jumping down there!" she snapped. "Are you insane?"

"You *are* jumping," he said calmly. "Unless you wish to meet my brother and your mafia friends, who are undoubtedly waiting for us right now, at the end of that jetway."

Frowning up at her when Lia only stood there, gripping her coat in one hand and the doorway with the other, Loki exhaled impatiently.

"Come, come," the god said. "I will catch you. I thought that was implied, with my holding my hands up… as if I were about to catch you."

"You can't catch me!"

He rolled his eyes. "I assure you, I *can* catch you, and

quite easily. Jump now, little elf. Or we will never get to your sister in time. My brother will likely go there next, if he figures out who you are, and that you are with me. Unlike your mafia friends, he may not simply assume we switched planes in Bangkok... although I did my best to leave a confusing trail back at the airport there, buying multiple tickets and so forth."

Lia stared down at him, still fighting disbelief.

She couldn't really trust him to *catch* her, could she?

At the end of a thirty-foot drop?

Then she thought about Maia.

If Gregor thought she'd double-crossed him, God only knew what he'd do to Maia, or where he might take her.

Taking a deep breath, she closed her eyes.

Not letting herself think about how insane this was, what she was doing, or who she was letting herself trust, she threw herself out the open doorway. When she hit the warm air of Los Angeles, and gravity caught hold of her, she let out a strangled yelp.

It seemed like she fell, dropping like a stone, her heart lodged somewhere in her throat, for only a fraction of a second—

—when strong arms caught her, gripping her with hands made of iron, cradling her against an equally dense chest. The force of her landing made all of her breath leave her lungs in a shocked *whoosh*—

But it didn't hurt.

Somehow, despite the muscle on his arms, nothing about him hurt, either.

Gasping, Lia opened her eyes, staring up at that familiar face as he placed her back down on her feet, grinning at her.

"Light as a leaf, my dear," he said, bending down and kissing her cheek. "Of course, now you've got me all hot and bothered again, since I could see all the way up that naughty dress of yours as you fell."

Winking, he took her hand as she tugged the dress down her thighs as far as it would go. She stumbled after him, still barefoot, when he began to walk. Tying back her hair with a hair-band she found in her coat pocket as she walked, she picked her steps carefully as he led her on a zig-zagging route under the plane.

He managed to sneak them past the baggage handlers tossing luggage out a lower access point in the middle of the fuselage, taking them around and back until they were under the jetway, and presumably invisible from the airport windows.

Loki had them follow that all the way under the concourse itself, and into a maintenance area filled with loading and emergency vehicles. Lia followed him, watching him grip her satchel at his waist. She buttoned up her long coat so she wouldn't feel completely naked, running fast on bare feet across the asphalt as Loki led them out of the airport and towards the street.

He eventually brought them around to the front of the building, where he found them a taxi stand.

He must have done something to mess with the other people in line for a taxi, because Lia found herself standing at the front of the line with him, holding the receipt of another person who'd been standing there a few seconds before.

Loki had taken the receipt off the guy and shooed him away, and Lia watched the man wander back through the crowd of people queued up for taxis and to the row of taxi-ordering kiosks, clearly confused, his expression puzzled.

He left his suitcase at the curb.

Lia frowned at Loki, who only winked at her in return.

"What about karma?" she said, her voice a touch accusing.

"Perks of being a god, love," he said, giving her a sideways smile. "I pick my karmic battles, just like any other being. Speaking of which, shall we take his suitcase? See if he has anything interesting inside? He seems like the type who might have a lot of women's underwear... along with some nasty porn and a giant dildo with a fist at the end."

Lia snorted a laugh, in spite of herself.

Looking down at the suitcase as their cab pulled up to the curb, she hesitated.

Then, after another brief hesitation, she shrugged, grabbing the handle and dragging it into the back of the taxi cab with them.

No reason to look a gift horse in the mouth.

She was a *thief,* after all.

8

A LITTLE BAD

Contrary to Loki's predictions, Lia didn't find any dildos in the suitcase they stole, or any illegal pornography. She didn't find any ladies' underwear, either.

She did find *men's* clothes, which was hardly surprising.

She also found three bottles of expensive Scotch.

Oh, and a hell of a lot of cash.

There was enough cash tucked away in that suitcase, in fact, that Lia wondered if he'd brought it into the country illegally, maybe by neglecting to declare the amount via his U.S. customs form. She estimated he had around twenty-five grand there, in taped-up stacks of one-hundred-dollar bills.

After she did her best to estimate how much was there, she left half in the suitcase for Loki, and put the other half in her satchel, which Loki had given back to her. She also took an expensive sports-watch she found, some gold cufflinks, and one bottle of the aged Scotch.

Meanwhile, she'd already taken out her boots and socks, and put them on her feet.

She offered the suitcase to Loki after she'd done her

assessment, pulling her boots out of her satchel to make room for the money and scotch, and putting those and the socks back on her feet. Loki went through the suitcase while she laced up her boots.

She saw him glance at the money, then open one of the two bottles of Scotch after staring at the label, and take a long drink.

Then he shooed her with her fingers to get the thing away from him.

Shrugging, Lia pulled out the rest of the twenty-five grand and put it inside her satchel, just barely squeezing it into her overstuffed bag. She managed in part by transferring some of her clothes, which needed replacing anyway, into the man's suitcase.

Zipping up the bag, she ripped the ID tags off it and dragged it out of the taxi when they stopped, only to leave it on the curb in downtown Santa Monica.

A few blocks later, she dumped the ID tags in a trash receptacle.

She figured someone would get some use out of the clothes, at least.

And hopefully the suitcase.

And the last bottle of Scotch.

She'd given Loki Gregor's address, which was in Malibu.

When Loki told the taxi driver an address in Santa Monica instead, she figured he wanted to change taxis to confuse their trail. For the same reason, she was a little bewildered when he got out of the taxi and simply walked down the street, beckoning her to come along.

From the way he scanned the sidewalks, he definitely appeared to be looking for something.

Whatever it was, it wasn't another taxi.

Lia saw his eyes light up when they'd gone about two blocks.

She stopped dead, watching as Loki walked right up to a steel-gray and sky-blue Bugatti Divo, which had just pulled up to the curb in front of them. Loki walked to the driver's side, bending down to lean his forearms on the open window.

Lia watched, incredulous, as Loki chatted with the Bugatti's gray-haired driver for a few seconds, right before he straightened, turning to her and waving her over.

"Come, darling," the god drawled. "This nice man has agreed to give us his car."

She fought not to laugh.

She only half-succeeded.

Still, her primary reaction remained disbelief.

Even after watching Loki pull this crap multiple times now, not to mention all the glamouring he'd done to people in the Bangkok airport and on both planes, Lia couldn't help staring as the gray-haired man got out of his car, and handed Loki the keys.

After bowing formally to the God of Mischief, the gray-haired man proceeded to walk away from his car with a smile on his face, like he didn't have a care in the world. Lia happened to know a Bugatti like that cost more, new, than most people's houses—even in Los Angeles, even in Santa Monica.

Hell, even in Beverly Hills.

Anyone watching would have assumed the man worked for Loki. It looked like the gray-haired man just got the car detailed and was now returning it to its rightful owner.

As Lia walked around to the passenger side of the car, the gray-haired man waved to her in a friendly way, glancing down her in the form-fitting white dress, which was visible again since she'd unfastened the front of her green leather coat.

Lia didn't bother to wave back.

She watched Loki climb into the driver's seat, but not

before the god gave her one of his shark-like grins, blowing her a kiss.

"Get in, sweets," he called out, loud enough that a few people on the sidewalk turned, staring at them. "And pull up your dress. I want to stroke your cunt while we drive. And I plan to drive fast, so there's no time to waste."

Snorting a laugh, Lia rolled her eyes.

She knew he said it primarily for shock value, and maybe to embarrass her. Maybe for the same reason, she found herself more amused than appalled.

"You're a pervy weirdo," she told him, equally loud. "And an exhibitionist."

He only winked, grinning wider.

"You know it, baby."

She snorted at that, too.

Tossing her satchel in the back and climbing into the passenger seat after he unlocked and opened her door, she couldn't help grinning with him after he inserted the car key and flipped on the ignition, hitting the gas to rev a motor that positively roared, vibrating pleasantly under her seat.

"Oooh," she said, smiling as she wriggled in the leather upholstery. "Maybe I could get used to this."

"Get used to it, darling," he grinned at her. "You're a god's bitch now."

Again, Lia couldn't help it.

She laughed.

⊙⊰⊗

L oki pulled into Gregor's driveway without slowing, barreling down the long, winding, white cement drive at around sixty miles per hour.

Feeling her nerves climb, her heart inching its way up into her throat for the first time since they successfully left the airport, Lia held onto the window frame and the Bugatti's dashboard, giving Loki a sideways look and a frown as he gunned it even faster over the hill leading to the cliffside mansion.

"This is subtle," she informed him.

Loki glanced at her, and she quirked an eyebrow.

"I thought we'd be a little more... you know... ninja-like. For a kidnapping."

"No time for that, my dear," he informed her, laying a heavy hand on her thigh and massaging the long muscle there. "It's not like he won't know who's behind this. For the same reason, covert ops are hardly going to gain us much."

Thinking about that, Lia tilted her head, conceding his point.

Gregor would definitely know she was involved.

If Maia disappeared, Gregor would have exactly one suspect.

It's not like soulless, sociopathic Mommy Dearest was around to give a shit.

Loki glanced at her, his eyebrows rising to his hairline.

"Ouch," he said.

She thumped his arm. "Ouch what?"

"You will tell me this story, yes, little elf?" He pushed at her with his own hand, then grabbed her thigh again, yanking her closer to where he sat, despite the gear shift between them. "About your mother and how you ended up owing this dreadful man?"

Lia frowned.

After a pause, she shrugged.

No reason *not* to tell him, given everything.

"There's not much of a story," she admitted. "Our mom stole from Gregor. Gregor took my sister as collateral. I work for Gregor. End of story."

"Hmm." Loki looked at her, obviously unsatisfied by her

truncated version of events. "How much did Mummy Dearest steal?"

"Dunno. Gregor says upwards of ten million."

Loki whistled, smiling humorlessly as he shook his head. "And she did not bring you along? That seems rather... evil. If you don't mind my saying."

"You would know," she teased.

He gave her a sharper look.

"I am not *evil,* precious." He sniffed a little, as if offended. "Even my brother Thor would concede that much. I may not be the boy scout he is, but I would *never* leave an offspring in the hands of someone like this Gregor. I would peel his skin off in small strips if he stole one of my children. Furthermore... I am not *evil,* little elf."

He gave her another look.

"A little bad, perhaps. A little difficult. But not evil."

Lia frowned, but mostly in her mind, not where he would see it. If she didn't know better, she'd think she'd really offended him.

"Perhaps you did," he grunted.

She opened her mouth to answer, but Loki waved her off.

"Finish your story," he demanded. "Hurry now. We are here."

He pulled up in front of the enormous, white-stone house, with the nymph-filled marble fountain in the center of the driveway.

Loki drove right up to the front door, then drove past it, parking on the other side of the loop. Slowing the car at the edge of the lawn, he drove carefully out onto the grass to get the Bugatti off the paved surface, coming to a stop maybe thirty feet from the front door.

The god activated the parking brake, and switched off the ignition.

Turning in his seat, he looked at her, his arm on the steering wheel.

"Okay," the god said, motioning towards her with a hand. "Tell me now. Quickly. And then I will go get your sister."

"We can't just sit here," she said, frowning. Lia motioned up at the house. "He has guards. People watching us."

"They will not see us. Not yet. And we still have some time before there is much risk of others arriving here, from the airport or elsewhere. Tell me."

Lia blinked. "Tell you what?"

"The rest of your story."

Lia frowned.

Then, realizing Loki wasn't going to leave until she told him more, she exhaled, combing her blond hair out of her face where it had fallen out of the ponytail.

"My mom did for Gregor what I now do for Gregor. Well, with one exception," she added sourly. "My mom provided a few 'extra services' that I've been unwilling to do for him, regardless of how much money he's tried to throw at me."

Grimacing, she gave Loki a sideways look.

"Gregor keep hinting, pretty obnoxiously, frankly, that he intends for me to eventually take him up on his offer. It's a lot of money," she admitted. "But I just can't bring myself to do it. I admit, it would probably make our lives easier in some ways, but I can't stand the thought of Maia being trapped in that house a day longer than necessary. Also, Maia told me, flat-out, that she would never forgive me."

Sighing, she combed a hand through her hair again.

"I don't think I'd forgive myself," she added. "And frankly, it would probably just put me in more of a cage with him. And Maia. He might never let us go."

Loki's green eyes darkened.

"Continue," he said, his voice colder.

"So, yeah, my mom and Gregor had a relationship," Lia

said, shrugging. "If you could call it that." Folding her arms, she motioned up towards the beachside mansion. "I've been coming to this house since I was a kid. Maybe only a few years older than my sister is now. I remember watching Gregor and my mom make out while we played in the pool. Sometimes Gregor's thugs would take us down to the beach to give them 'grownup time.'"

Lia shuddered, grimacing again.

"But your mother was also a thief," Loki clarified.

Lia nodded, sighing.

"She worked as an 'acquisitions expert' for Gregor." Lia made air quotes around the title with her fingers. "For his 'import-export' business."

"What did she steal?" Loki said. "What do *you* steal?"

Lia shrugged, still hugging her arms.

"Information, mostly," she said. "Sometimes more cat-burglary type stuff. Expensive art. Sometimes jewelry. That kind of thing. More and more lately, it's been bigger-stakes stuff. Even some government and military-type things."

"What were you in Kathmandu to steal?"

"Information," Lia said, sighing.

She motioned towards the house a second time.

"Loki, he has people in and out of here all the time. Guards who walk the perimeter. Guards on the roof who would have seen us come down the driveway. Are you absolutely certain no one could have seen us come in here?"

"Yes. I am certain." Loki studied her face, frowning. "I glamoured the car right before we pulled into the driveway. Continue, little elf."

Exhaling again, Lia shrugged.

"I was in Kathmandu to get information on what a rich guy in the Chinese government planned to do with banking policy in Southeast Asia." Looking over at Loki, she smiled. "Sexy, huh?"

"Did you succeed?" Loki queried.

Lia gave him a wan smile. "Of course."

"How did you do that?"

"I bugged his hotel," Lia said, shrugging. "I picked him up in the bar, wearing something a lot hotter than what you met me in, and bugged the collar of his suit jacket. I tried to get into the Chinese Embassy, but I couldn't pull that off without risking getting ID'd."

Lia shrugged, glancing out the window at one of the armed guards on the roof of Gregor's mansion.

"It didn't matter that much in the end. Between the bug on his suit and a prostitute I sent his way, I got more than enough. Enough that Gregor likely would have been very pleased with my results."

Sighing, she refolded her arms, adding,

"I was lucky, really. The guy liked to talk when he drank. I got a number of pretty detailed discussions between Gregor's corrupt government contact and several other Chinese banking executives who were discussing their holdings in different parts of Asia, including Nepal, India, Thailand, Singapore. Deals they cut with mafias in different parts of the world. Money laundering. Trafficking. Bribery. Hours of recordings. Not to mention video of him with the prostitute and several of her friends... he's married to the daughter of some bigwig in the Party, so I suspect that would've helped Gregor out even more."

"I see."

Loki smiled at her.

Lia swore she saw a hint of pride in his eyes as he looked her over.

"Very impressive, my darling," he added. "What else?"

"What else?" She frowned at him, puzzled.

"About your mother."

Lia sighed, letting her head fall to the cushioned car seat.

"I don't know what you're waiting to hear, Loki. My mom was a piece of shit, working for an even bigger piece of shit. She was skimming. She was pretending to fuck up acquisitions and selling product herself, cutting the Syndicate out of it. She was also double-selling some of the intel Gregor was having her steal, often to rival corporations or governments. Meaning whatever lowlife Gregor already had a contract with, she'd sell it to the other guy, or even to a third party. Eventually, her double-dipping got around. Gregor was *furious*."

At Loki's quirked eyebrow, she added,

"Gregor might be a petty, piece of shit thug, but he understands the importance of reputation in business... even this business. If the other corrupt lowlifes can't trust you, they won't buy from you. Gregor had to convince them he could still be trusted. He had to convince them he'd taken care of her, that it would never happen again. He more or less paraded me around for that very reason, letting them think he'd turned me into his personal slave. Even then, he lost clients. My mom was... is... really beautiful. People said she used sex to manipulate Gregor, making him a chump. Some clients left just because they were pissed. Well-paying clients. Influential clients."

"Ah." The god nodded. "I see. Most understandable. Pray continue. This story is *very* interesting."

Thinking, staring up at the roof of the car, Lia shrugged.

"What more is there to say? Gregor blamed mom not just for what she stole but for the clients he lost... and for making him look like a fool. Dear old mum didn't clue us in on what she was doing. When she got caught, she just bailed. That was five years ago, and I still have no idea where she went. She more or less vanished... and with every cent of the money she'd stolen from Gregor. He never got any of it back."

Lia turned her head, giving Loki a grim look.

"But Gregor found us. Me and Maia. I was going to

college at Santa Barbara. His muscle showed up at my dorm room and more or less kidnapped me in broad daylight, with guns to my head. Gregor already had Maia with him. At his house."

Lia motioned with her jaw towards the mansion behind them.

"...This house."

Loki frowned.

"You mother did not warn you?"

Lia let out a bitter laugh. "Are you kidding? She knew Gregor had all of our phones tapped. He didn't trust anyone. It's part of why he was so pissed."

Her voice grew bitter as she adjusted her back in the seat, adding,

"I can forgive what she did to me. But Mom just *left* Maia there. Alone. At her place in Los Feliz. Maia doesn't even remember how long she sat there, waiting for mom to come back from her latest 'trip,' before Gregor's goons showed up. Days. Probably over a week. She sat in an empty house, alone, playing video games for days. Watching Netflix. Eating things like potato chips and ramen and canned fruit until she ran out. She eventually went to the neighbors when she got too hungry. She was afraid to call me because she knew I'd be furious with mom. She didn't want to get our mom in trouble."

Lia's back molars ground together.

"...She was seven years old."

Loki quirked an eyebrow, frowning.

"And she's never once contacted you?" he said. "Your mother? No cryptic messages on your little machine? No note spelled out in refrigerator magnets or cut up newspapers?"

Lia shook her head, exhaling.

"Nope."

"Well, well." Loki's frown deepened.

Lia was surprised to see real anger in the god's eyes.

"Shall we find her next, after this?" he said, his voice a touch harder. "Your mother? I would be interested in having a few words with her. I have... questions."

"No." Lia let out a humorless sound, half-laugh, half grunt of horror. "Absolutely not. Thank you for the offer, but *hell* no. I never want to see that train-wreck again. The only good thing that came of this is that she's out of our lives forever."

"You are certain?" Loki said.

He met her gaze, his green eyes perfectly still, like mirrored glass.

From the rage she sensed simmering there, she found herself thinking the offer was one hundred percent serious.

"...I would *really* like to speak with her, as I said," he added.

Smiling at him, in spite of herself, she laid a hand on his arm.

"No, honey," she said, caressing his skin, then leaning up impulsively to kiss him on the mouth. "But thank you."

Loki flinched.

Then he looked down at her hand on him, and her fingers.

He stared long enough that Lia was about to remove her hand, thinking perhaps she'd crossed some kind of boundary with him. She was about to withdraw her fingers when he suddenly caught them in his, bringing her palm up to his lips.

Kissing her hand, then her fingers, tenderly that time, he smiled at her.

"I like you very much, Lia Winchester," he said seriously.

She smiled wider. "Do you, now?"

"I do."

Thinking about that, she felt her smile fade.

"What you did to the driver," she said, watching his eyes. "The man who owned this." She indicated around at the

Bugatti Divo. "The man at the taxi stand. And the stewardesses."

Lia hesitated, studying his green eyes, wondering if he would tell her the truth if she asked. Wondering if she would know if he was lying.

Worse, wondering if she could bear to watch him lie if she did know.

"Yes?" Loki lifted that eyebrow, giving her a faintly wicked smile. "Is there something you wish to ask me, my darling, sexy, utterly adorable little elf?"

Lia hesitated a beat longer.

Finally, she resolved herself.

She opened her mouth to speak, but he cut her off.

"No," he said.

He stripped the humor from his voice, leaving it hard as metal.

"...Absolutely not," he added. "No, Lia. Never."

She flinched, then frowned.

"What question are you answering?" she said, skeptical.

"No, I never did that to you," he said. "NO, I never messed with your mind, or glamoured you, apart from masquerading as that old woman on the plane. NO, I never convinced you to do something you would not have otherwise done. No, I never did to you what I did to them. NO, I never coerced you in some dishonest way to let me fuck you."

He stared at her eyes, his green eyes serious, verging on guileless.

Squeezing her hand where he continued to hold it in his, he added,

"I'm not even convinced it would work on you at this point, little elf. I'm beginning to think you may have god's blood in your ancestry somewhere. You are far too clever and perceptive for your own good, even if you *are* a full-blooded human."

At Lia's frown, he grinned.

"No, dummy," he said, louder, pushing at her shoulder playfully, the way she had with him. "No, no, no. NO. I do not force ANYONE into sex with me. Never. Absolutely never. My pride would never allow it. I certainly don't do it to pretty elves I have a horrendous crush on, especially ones who suck my cock in dressing rooms... and let me dress them in slutty clothes just so I may molest them more easily... and allow me to fuck them in all manner of perverted ways on commercial airplanes filled with human passengers..."

"Never?" she said, skeptical, raising an eyebrow of her own.

"Never," he affirmed. "I told you... a *little* bad. Not evil."

The frown continued to toy at her lips.

Strangely, though, it wasn't because she didn't believe him.

It was because she did.

9

SISTERS

Lia bit her lip, staring into the rearview mirror at the enormous beachfront house behind her.

She was seated on the driver's side of the Bugatti Divo, waiting for Loki, who'd disappeared inside the mansion. She stared at the front door, willing him to reappear. Willing him to come back out, for him to have Maia with him, for both of them to be okay.

Her eyes darted to the clock on the dash.

She looked up to the roof, at the men holding semi-automatic rifles.

She looked back at the front door.

It was way too damned quiet.

But Loki told her to wait here.

He told her to get into the driver's seat once he was gone, and wait for him.

He told her he would be right back.

That was at least thirty minutes ago.

She was beyond worried.

She was worried as hell about her baby sister, Maia.

She was worried, God help her, about Loki.

She was worried he'd been caught, or shot, or worse.

She stared at the mansion's front door, willing it to open, even as some part of her strained for any sound, looking for any irregularity, any change in the guards overhead that would give her some indication of what was going on inside those walls.

The guards looked the same, however. And most of what Lia heard was the sound of the ocean coming from either side of the rocky, tree-covered cliff. She heard the wind, birds in the sky, the distant sound of a television.

There was nothing else.

Until suddenly, there was.

Gunshots.

Two of them—one right after the other.

Lia jumped in her seat, panting. She turned around entirely in the leather seat, staring through the back window at the front of the mansion.

The red-painted, enormous door remained closed.

Lia turned back to face front, looking at the side mirror closest to her, which she'd tilted at an angle that allowed her to see the guards on the roof.

For the first time, she saw a change there, too.

They were all gone.

The roof was empty.

Lia sat there, panting, listening for more sounds.

The problem was, the only sounds she could think of that would actually tell her anything about what was going on inside were bad sounds.

More gunfire. Screams. Explosions.

She didn't hear any of that, not now, but once was enough.

Cursing under her breath, Lia yanked on the silver handle located on the inside of the panel to open the Bugatti's driver's-side door. Pushing the door the rest of the way open with her hand and leg, she got out, looked around, then made a run for the front door of the house.

She found it unlocked and didn't wait, turning the handle and pushing it open, poking her head in and peering around.

No one.

The entryway was entirely empty.

She didn't hear footsteps upstairs. She didn't see anyone on the long deck visible through the bay windows below the foyer. The sunken living room just past the entryway was empty, too, right in front of the massive window overlooking the Pacific.

The whole ocean-facing side of the house, including the windows in the living room, jutted out in the shape of a triangle, like the prow of a massive ship. Out on the deck itself, Lia saw a fire pit, a jacuzzi, blue and white deck furniture, a number of fountains.

It might have been nice, if it belonged to anyone else.

Closing the front door quietly behind her, she crept forward, checking out the rest of the living room and bar, both of which were visible to her once she'd crept past the mirrored walls of the entryway. The cathedral ceiling stretched above, but Lia's view of that continued to be obstructed somewhat by the floor above, and the carpeted stairs, which started on the right side of the foyer.

Everything looked empty.

The house was silent.

Lia knew the basic layout of the house, just from coming here with her mom as she was growing up. Gregor's office, the kitchen, dining room, and two living rooms were downstairs. So was the security station, a gym, an entertainment room, and a small private theater.

All the bedrooms were upstairs.

So was a second study, a sex-dungeon playroom Lia had the misfortune of stumbling upon once, while she was still in high school, and a second common area with a small wet bar and some pool tables.

Cocking her head, Lia listened, trying to decide which direction to go.

It struck her how foolhardy this was.

She should have waited for Loki in the car.

There was no point coming in here if she had no idea where Loki was, or where Maia was, or what Loki's plan had been to get both of them out. For all Lia knew, Loki might have cased the whole place already, and not found Maia anywhere inside the building.

Maia could be down by the pool.

Maia could also be down on the beach.

Lia remembered playing down there a lot when she was in high school, entertaining baby Maia and waiting for her mom to "finish up" with Gregor in the house.

Hell, Gregor might have taken Maia with him to the airport.

He might even have done it as a reward for Lia, since he thought Lia was bringing him the windfall of Loki and the ring.

Grimacing at the thought, Lia stood in the entryway, trying to decide what to do.

She was about to back slowly out of the house—

When she heard a car approaching outside, on the driveway.

Feeling every muscle in her body clench, Lia turned her head, staring out the clear glass squares that formed slightly-warped windows on either side of the front door. Through those squares, she saw a caravan of cars heading down the white-paved driveway towards her, and towards the house she'd just broken into.

Panting, Lia watched the cars with their blacked-out windows as they stopped all around the driveway. She flinched as the doors started to open, expelling a lot of men. Over half of those men wore regular street clothes, despite the fancy cars with their chrome fronts and blacked-out windows. Several wore sports jerseys over jeans, with only a few wearing more expensive suits and designer outfits that made her think of Eurotrash club-wear from the nineties.

Gregor's guys.

Lia recognized most of them.

She knew a lot of them by name.

Holding her breath, she waited, staring around at the crowd of forms, looking to see if Maia came out of any of those vehicles. She only saw a single female in that entire sea of male bodies and faces, and Lia recognized her, too.

Maria Velacruz was one of Gregor's lawyers and oldest personal friends.

The woman was also pushing sixty.

Definitely not Lia's twelve-year-old sister.

Then Lia saw a man get out of the middle car, wearing a full Armani suit, dark gray, with a black shirt and a black square in his front lapel pocket.

He buttoned the suit jacket as he stepped out of the back of a Rolls-Royce someone else had been driving, gazing up at his mansion, a hard frown on his face.

Gregor.

She had no trouble recognizing that salt-and-pepper curly hair, the full mouth, the pale skin, the rings he wore on four of his fingers.

She knew Gregor Farago was Hungarian or something like that, but he looked so much like a mobster out of a movie, from his clothes down to the way he spoke, his hand gestures and those dumb sunglasses he was always wearing, she forgot and made him Greek or Italian in her mind, somewhere Mediterranean.

Unfortunately, Lia knew that face, though.

She knew it well enough to recognize the exact expression Gregor wore, even with the dark wraparound shades obscuring his eyes.

Gregor was murderous.

She watched her "boss" tug down the edges of his suit jacket, then follow three of his men towards the front door of his house.

Feeling her breath start to stall and hitch in her chest, Lia turned back towards the interior of the house, trying to decide what to do.

She was still standing there, half-paralyzed, when she heard a scream.

The scream came from inside the house.

It was a girl's scream.

A heartbreakingly familiar scream.

Lia heard it echo over her head, and knew it came from upstairs.

She didn't think.

Turning on her heel, she darted across the foyer, running up the carpeted stairs two at a time in her furred boots. She dashed down the hallway at the top of the stairs, aiming her feet for a row of doors she knew as bedrooms, including the one where she'd slept in high school, the same one where her sister had been sleeping for the past five years, ever since their mother abandoned them.

Lia ran, all-out, for that room now.

As it turned out, her instincts were good—accurate, at least.

Lia stopped in the doorway, grabbing the wood frame in both hands as she stared inside, panting. The scene greeting her eyes confused her at first, alarmed her, then infuriated her, then alarmed her all over again as she took in the three people inside her old bedroom.

She found Loki with her eyes first.

She felt nothing but relief when her new god-boyfriend appeared to be all right.

She couldn't say the same for the man currently *with* Loki, but honestly, Lia couldn't have cared less about him. He definitely wasn't Lia's priority.

Her eyes swung around the rest of the room then, searching for Maia.

She found her in a matter of seconds.

Her kid sister Maia, twelve years old, was crammed into the opposite corner of the room from Loki and his new "friend," in the crevice behind a twin bed with unicorn sheets, and only a few yards away from Lia. The bed, which was covered in fluffy pink and white pillows, and a unicorn comforter, had been pushed into an odd angle, almost like someone had trapped her back there, behind the bed.

Or maybe like they'd put her there for safekeeping, moving the bed to shield her.

Maia sat on the floor, her knees bent, her eyes too round in her face.

She was staring across the room, where Loki was dealing with the other person in the room, an enormous man Lia knew.

Ernie.

Ernie worked for Gregor, and was pretty high up in his inner circle from what Lia knew. She had no idea if Ernie was his real name. Everyone called him Ernie, either because it actually was his name or because he had a bizarre habit of wearing shirts with horizontal black, orange, and yellow stripes, making him look like the Muppet character of Burt and Ernie fame.

Unlike the Muppet, this Ernie was built like a tank.

Each of his arms was bigger than both of Lia's legs put together.

He had an enormous barrel chest, a sagging gut, thick legs, huge hands.

Juxtaposed with his size was a strangely young-looking, baby-round face.

Between his shape and the clothes he wore, he'd always looked like an oversized toddler to Lia, although he had to be in his late thirties, at least. As long as she'd known him, Lia always thought he looked like the offspring of some kind of fairytale ogre.

Right now, Ernie wasn't having a good day.

Loki was slamming the big man's head against the wall.

Repeatedly.

Not at all gently.

He was slamming it hard enough, Ernie's skull had already worn a hole in the paint and the sheetrock below, and was now connecting with a solid *thunk* with the wooden, two-by-four stud that lived under the paint and sheetrock.

As Loki slammed the man's head into the wall, he muttered angrily under his breath.

At first, Lia didn't understand him. She heard him muttering words in some other language, something she didn't recognize.

Then he switched to English, and she understood perfectly.

As she did, the rage she'd felt when first seeing her sister bloomed back in her chest.

"We... do... not... touch... children..." Loki growled, slamming the man's head harder. "We... do... not... *think*... about... touching... children. We... do... not... dress... children... in... adult... only... clothing..."

Lia's jaw clenched until it hurt.

She looked at Maia again, and, more to the point, at what she was wearing.

Her hands clenched into fists as she fought to suppress her rage.

Then she ran for her.

"MAIA!"

She more or less screamed her name.

The horror and fury she'd been suppressing exploded out of her, so intensely she couldn't think straight, could barely breathe. Lia shoved the bed out of the way, running for her sister, feeling her horror deepen when she saw the rest of what her sister wore.

Someone had painted her face with gaudy, burlesque-style, clown make-up.

She had rouge on her cheeks, blue and gold glitter eyeshadow, thick eyeliner and mascara, red lipstick, a beauty mark on one cheek. She wore fishnet stockings, a teddy with silk boxer shorts that barely covered the top of her thighs, and six-inch heels.

Lia threw herself down, wrapping her arms around her sister, and Maia clutched at her, staring at her like she wasn't sure if Lia herself was real.

"Lia?" she said, her voice tremulous.

"Yes. Yes, yes, yes. We're getting you out of here. Now. I promise."

"Is that guy really with you? He said he was."

Lia's head turned, her eyes finding Loki where he continued to smack Ernie's head into the wooden stud through the hole in the sheetrock.

"Yes," she said, her voice holding a fierce kind of approval, what verged on full-blown pride. "Yes. He is definitely with me."

Lia was still crushing her little sister against her when Loki's voice rose.

His words were loud, but utterly calm.

Something about them immediately relaxed the worst of the terror in Lia's chest, even before she made full sense of his actual words.

"Yes, I am with her," Loki called out, his voice as hard as metal. He turned, meeting Lia's gaze from across the room. "I am sorry you had to see this, my darling, but do not worry, little elf!" Loki glared at the man slumped below him, now bleeding from the head as he leaned against the bedroom wall. "This enormous piece of dinosaur excrement did not touch your sister, despite how it may appear. He certainly wanted to. He certainly was working his way up to it... weren't you, you sack of mouse testes?"

Lia's voice shook.

"Are you sure?" she said, gripping Maia tighter.

"I am very sure. This is him escalating things, apparently, after clumsy attempts to woo her. Your sister tells me this is the first time he's gone this far, however."

"This far?" Lia said, her voice growing shrill. "What is *this far*, exactly?"

"He photographed her. He gave her the clothes and instructed her to paint her face... but that is all. We got here in the nick of time, it seems."

Loki turned, glaring at Ernie, who was still slumped against the wall, holding his bleeding head in one hand.

He was blubbering like a giant child now, snot running down his face.

"He had it all worked out, though, didn't you, my disgusting pile of rotted Fangor vomit?" Letting out a low growl, Loki kicked the large man in the gut. "He was thinking about it. He was plotting. He was planning how to hurt this poor little mouse. Weren't you? Weren't you? You giant sack of maggot-infested boar entrails?"

Loki kicked him again, and the man threw up his hands,

whining as he pushed himself backwards, scooting down the wall with his butt and legs, trying to get away.

Loki's words finally reached her mind.

Or maybe Lia just finally believed them.

She turned to Maia, staring into her face.

"Is that true?" she said. "Tell me the truth, Maia. Is what you told Loki true?"

Maia nodded.

She looked past Lia, her eyes finding the huge man scrunched against the wall. The man was still crying quietly as he stared up at Loki, fear in his eyes.

"He's been creepy for a while," Maia said, looking back at Lia. "But he didn't touch me."

She looked at Lia's dress then, which was now visible under the open leather coat.

"What the heck are *you* wearing?" Maia demanded.

Lia flushed, drawing away so she could pull the leather coat closed, buttoning the front.

"Go get changed," Lia said, climbing back to her feet and pointing at the walk-in closet. "Fast as you can. We have to go. Now."

Maia ran for her closet.

Once she'd disappeared inside, Lia looked at Loki.

"Gregor's downstairs," she said. "He pulled up with his whole entourage right before I came up here—"

"I know, pet. I know." Loki held up a hand. "It's quite all right."

"Where are the rest of them?" Lia demanded. "The guards? I saw all of them on the roof, then nothing."

"They're taking a little nap right now, lover. Never fear. They won't wake up until we are long gone."

Lia scowled. "What about the gunshots I heard?"

"One guard made it down here early," the god said with a

dismissive wave. "I was a little preoccupied, and didn't hear him. My own fault, really."

Lia bit her lip, folding her arms. "And the gunshots?"

Loki shrugged, glancing at the wall behind him. Lia's eyes followed the direction of his pointing finger, seeing two bullet holes, one roughly Loki's chest-height, and the other roughly the height of Loki's head.

"Were those meant for you?" she said accusingly.

Loki shrugged again, smiling.

"He missed."

Before Lia could answer that time, Maia opened the closet door.

She emerged wearing blue jeans and a pink T-shirt with a beaded heart on the front. Lia exhaled in relief as she watched Maia shove an arm into a dark-blue, zip-up, hoodie sweatshirt, holding a washcloth in her other hand.

She'd obviously been rubbing the washcloth on her face.

The yellow terrycloth was already smeared with red lipstick and rouge, beige foundation, black eyeliner, and baby-blue glitter eyeshadow.

Looking past her little sister, through the door of the closet, Lia realized she'd forgotten a bathroom lived on the other side.

Maia finished hiking the sweatshirt up on her shoulders, stomping down on her heels to get her Vans to settle on her socked feet. Once she had her clothes fully situated, she rubbed the washcloth on her face a few more times, scrubbing her skin more vigorously before she tossed the cloth down to the carpeted floor.

"Let's get out of here," Maia said, sounding impatient. "Can we go? You came to rescue me, right? To get me out of here? So we should go. I could hear people downstairs."

Hearing the irritation and impatience and worry in Maia's voice, Lia felt another huge surge of relief. It sounded so much like her, so normal, so teen-agey, she felt that fear that had terrorized her chest slowly start to calm down.

Loki said the guy hadn't touched her.

Maia said the same.

She believed them.

Her sister was okay. She was going to be okay.

Even as the thoughts ran through Lia's mind, Maia turned, looking at Loki. Despite her scream earlier, and the fear Lia saw in her sister's eyes when she first came into the room, Maia clearly saw Loki differently now.

Lia could see it in her sister's eyes: Loki was now solidly in the friend/ally column.

Maybe it was seeing Lia, hearing from Lia's own mouth that Loki was on her team. Or maybe it was a combination of that and what Loki had done to Ernie.

Whatever the reason, Maia's fear of him was completely gone.

Lia followed the direction of her sister's stare.

Loki grinned at her, winking.

He directed his words at Maia, however.

"But of course, my little nunchuk... of course! We are *absolutely, one hundred percent* here to rescue you! And we can leave whenever you wish. Didn't your big sister tell you? When it comes to the Winchester women, I live to serve..."

10

DISTRACTION

Maia took to the idea that Loki could make them invisible far better than Lia would have expected.

Lia's younger sister barely asked either of them any questions.

More than anything, she just seemed to want out of there as quickly as possible, and given the small amount she'd seen, Lia could scarcely blame her.

Whatever her thinking, Maia followed the God of Mischief confidently, without question, seeming to trust him implicitly.

Truthfully, Lia found Maia's trust in Loki a little disorienting—not only because of the scream, but because of the god's near-constant teasing and the fact that Loki was a complete stranger to her. Maia did everything Loki told her to do, without hesitation, without complaint, without any visible doubt. She didn't make a sound as she crept after him down the carpeted corridor in her Vans, then down the carpeted stairs.

Within minutes, the three of them were back in the

mirrored foyer with the large front door, with the windows composed of glass bricks.

That's where things got a bit more complicated.

Lia, who took up the rear, glanced around nervously as she heard Gregor and his entourage talking downstairs in the living room.

The front door was open now, and guarded by two men on the front step.

Five more of Gregor's men milled in the foyer, and Loki pulled Maia easily sideways when one of them lumbered up the stairs, either to use the bathroom or to check on Maia. The three of them ended up crouched by a potted palm tree, with at least six enormous, male bodies standing directly between them and the car waiting for them outside.

"We need another way out," Lia muttered to Loki. "Whether they can see us or not, they're going to freak out if invisible people smack into them and knock them down. If that guy went upstairs looking for Ernie, or Maia, or both of them, they are going to freak when they find Maia missing... they'll probably case out all the airports. And if your brother is there—"

"Yes, yes, my darling girl." Loki kissed her mouth, smiling. "It'll be all right. I've got the Maia end covered for now. I knocked out the perverted oaf. They won't see him again until we are gone. And it will appear to them that your little dumpling is asleep in her unicorn bed. I put a bit of a repellent spell on her, as well, so they'll be reluctant to wake her..."

Trailing, and frowning a bit, he glanced around the foyer.

"We just need a bit of a distraction..." he muttered.

He looked around at the thick-necked men milling in the foyer, some in dark suits and some looking like they were part of a rapper's entourage, then to their right, down at the sunken living room, where voices continued to rise and fall.

After a few seconds, Loki seemed to make up his mind.

Reaching out with a hand, he flicked his fingers in the area of the living room.

Lia blinked, staring, when a whole human being appeared out of whole cloth. He blinked into existence without fanfare, without so much as an audible *pop*.

The new man stood in the exact center of the white-carpeted area directly in front of the leather couch where Gregor and several of his people sat.

For a brief instant, everyone in the living room froze, staring at the new person.

No one seemed to blink... or breathe.

It took Lia another blink herself to fully acknowledge the person there as real.

Well... as appearing real.

Basically, it took Lia a few seconds to realize that everyone else in Gregor's house was seeing the same figure there that she was.

The figure Loki conjured out of thin air was huge, a veritable mountain of muscle and broad shoulders, statuesque height and chiseled features.

His "bigness" contrasted strangely with Gregor's muscle-heads, in a way that took Lia a few seconds to comprehend. It wasn't just the clothes, although those were strange enough. It was something in the man's bearing, in his long, strawberry-blond hair that hung thickly down his back, his inhumanly handsome face, the stern look in his ice-blue eyes.

That, and Loki's vision didn't have an ounce of fat on him.

He dressed like some kind of Viking, with a thick, furred, white cape over an embroidered tunic and what looked like deerskin pants and boots. He gripped a silver hammer in one hand, with etched runes decorating the edges and a leather-wrapped handle.

The hammer seemed to glow with its own blue-white light.

Some of the glowing runes reminded Lia of the tattoos on Loki's upper chest.

It had to be Thor.

She had to be looking at a mirage of Loki's brother, Thor.

Next to her Maia's jaw was hanging.

"What the—?"

"Just a little light show, my dear," Loki assured her, patting Maia's shoulder. "Don't be alarmed, my little kumquat."

Below them, in the sunken living room, Gregor rose to his feet, right as guns rose, clutched in the hands of Gregor's muscle. Most of those guns were aimed at the giant Viking's chest, including a few shotguns and semi-automatic rifles.

"How did you get in here?" Gregor snapped.

The blond giant only smirked at him, raising the hammer to his shoulder.

Gregor's complexion darkened. "What in God's name are you wearing? Is this some sick joke? Because I said everything I had to say to you at the airport—"

"Back up!" one of Gregor's goons snarled, walking towards the Viking, aiming an automatic rifle at his gut.

Lia recognized him as Mike, one of Gregor's henchmen from way back.

"Back the fuck up, buddy... now. Right now."

Apparently, Maia needed a few seconds to adjust to the scene in the living room, as well. Now she turned her head, staring at Lia.

Then, seeming to see the confusion on her big sister's face, she turned to Loki.

"Who is that?" Maia whispered to Loki.

Loki turned his smile on her, lifting an eyebrow.

Despite the nearness of Gregor's men, some of whom were still only a scarce few feet away from them in the foyer, Loki answered Maia in his regular voice. From his casual tone, they might all be watching this unfold on television.

"That, my little chicken *momo* with spicy sauce, is my brother, Thor. Well..." Loki amended, tilting his head.

"...it is his *likeness,* anyway. Stripped of the more douche-y aspects of his personality, and a great deal less annoyingly full of recriminations and obnoxiously pious lectures. I thought it might be interesting to see how your mobster friends reacted to him. I wanted to ascertain if they'd spoken to him in the airport... which they clearly had. I am also curious if I can persuade them to react to my brother rather more *aggressively* the next time they see him. Were Thor to, say, show up here. In person, that is. For he definitely will..."

Loki glanced at Lia, quirking an eyebrow.

"...show up in person. As in soon. As in, he is on his way here now."

Both Lia and Maia turned to stare at him.

Both sisters were frowning, but for different reasons.

"Thor's coming here?" Lia said, alarmed.

Loki nodded grimly. "Yes. And rather quickly, I fear. I am now concerned he may have help. Rather formidable help."

"Help?" Lia said blankly. "What kind of help?"

"Help in the form of one of my other brothers," Loki replied.

Staring out the bay windows on the other side of the living room, the God of Mischief scowled at the thought, right before his eyes flickered back to the likeness of Thor. That likeness continued to glower from the center of the living room, posing menacingly with the hammer as Gregor continued to shout at him.

"...one of my *smarter* brothers," Loki concluded with a faint growl.

Maia, unlike her sister, was stuck on something else.

"You want Gregor to *shoot* your brothers?" she said, her voice openly shocked. "You want him and his goons to try to hurt your own brothers? Why?"

Loki glanced at her, his eyes showing him faintly startled.

"Oh, they can't *hurt* my brothers, my little chocolate Ho-Ho cupcake," Loki said, lifting an eyebrow. He smiled at her, patting her shoulder as his voice turned indulgent. "Your nasty kidnapper-mobster thug and his friends might *distract* my brothers a bit. Slow them down a little. Give us a bit of breathing room to get out of their immediate orbit... where they won't have such an easy time tracking me... but they can't actually *hurt* them."

Loki looked rather appalled at the thought.

"Why not?" Maia insisted.

Loki looked at her, winking.

He opened his mouth to answer her more fully, then turned his head as movement in the foyer distracted him. His pale eyes followed Gregor's no-necks as they began to move away from the front door, crushing their way into the sunken living room.

From the living room itself, the voices were getting noticeably more aggressive.

"Get out of here! Take him out, now!"

"Sir... we can't seem to move him."

"What do you mean you can't *move* him? I want him out of this room, at once! Throw him in the damned ocean, if you have to!"

Lia watched Gregor's men leave the area of the front door in bewilderment, even as it occurred to her that Gregor was back to yelling at the image of Thor, accusing it of somehow being involved with Lia's own disappearance.

It was completely bizarre to listen to Gregor yelling about her from less than fifty feet away, totally oblivious to the fact that Lia was standing right there, listening to every word.

"Where is she?" Gregor snapped. "I know you know where she is, you piece of shit. Did you poach my help? Offer her a sweet deal? Maybe promise to put her up in your Viking castle somewhere? Give her half your herd of oxen?"

A few of the goons chuckled at this, looking at one another.

Gregor didn't sound amused.

"Whatever she's offered you... whatever *sex* you've managed to get off her... trust me, it's not worth it. She's nothing but a lying, conniving whore, just like her mother. That whole family will bring you nothing but heartache."

Seeing the rage rise violently to Loki's eyes, Lia clutched at him in alarm.

She did it more in instinct than in thought, but her fingers stopped him, right as he'd been heading towards the living room.

The god halted his steps.

Turning his head, he looked at her. His green eyes glowed with that inhuman light she'd seen on him more than once. Now a cold fury lived there, within that mystical light, a depth of rage and intensity that briefly took her aback.

She touched his face, and Loki blinked.

He was looking at her again.

He was seeing *her* again.

"He's not worth it," Lia murmured, caressing his face. "The coast is clear. Your illusion worked. Let's blow this hotdog stand."

She motioned with her head towards the open door.

Only one of Gregor's goons remained outside.

After a brief pause, Loki frowned.

Then, aiming a last glare in the direction of Gregor, he took Lia's hand, leading her and Maia towards and through the open front door.

BROTHERS

L oki flipped the seat forward in the Bugatti, and
Maia crawled into the back, taking up residence in
the section of seat directly between theirs.

"You drive," the god told Lia, motioning her towards the
driver's side. "I might need to concentrate on other things."

Lia frowned a little, but didn't ask him to clarify.

She watched Loki look up at the sky, mystified when she
saw nothing but blue with a few small, white, cottony clouds.

"Tut-tut," Loki said, motioning at her again as he opened
the passenger-side door. "We mustn't dawdle, lover. Perhaps I
have not conveyed the depth of urgency, but we really, *really*
must hurry now."

Lia nodded.

Holding her coat closed over the white dress, she opened
the driver's-side door and got in, yanking her leather coat in
after her. Turning the key in the ignition as Loki got in beside
her and closed his door, Lia threw it in gear and stepped on
the gas, even as she glanced back at her sister, reaching her
hand back to briefly clasp her hand.

"I'm so happy you're with us," she said. "I'm so, so happy, Maia."

Her sister grinned back at her in the rearview mirror.

Her eyes grew brighter.

In those few seconds, it really hit Lia that Maia was with them.

She was out, she might even be free, and Maia was with them.

"I'm so happy to see you," Lia repeated, her own eyes stinging.

"Okay, okay," Maia said, wiping her eyes. She motioned towards the windshield with a wave of her hand. "Just don't be so happy you drive us all off a cliff. I want to get far enough away to do a *real* happy dance."

Lia nodded, but still found herself staring at her sister.

Twelve-year-old Maia looked thinner than Lia remembered, and too damned mature, even apart from the remnants of make-up and lipstick on her face. It was more the look Lia saw there, the observant-verging-on-wary expression in her sister's blue eyes.

It reminded her too much of herself.

Even so, Lia couldn't stop smiling. Tears stung her eyes above the shit-eating grin on her face. She released Maia's fingers to rest her hand on the gear shift, focusing back on the road as she wiped her cheeks and eyelashes with her fingers.

She maneuvered them forward off the grass lawn and around the other cars, leaving tire tracks and mud as she pulled the Bugatti Divo back out onto the white cement driveway. Once she'd straightened the car, she gunned it, aiming them for the first turn looping them up towards the Pacific Coast Highway, or PCH.

"Where are we going?" Maia said, poking her head

through the opening between their two seats. "You have a plan, right? You and your nutty friend?"

Maia looked at Loki fondly, then back at Lia.

"Can you believe what he did to Ernie?" she added, grinning wider. "That was AWESOME! You remember that jackass, right? He's been a total, lecherous jerk for the past few months... and he's worse whenever Gregor's not there. I think Gregor keeps him off me because of you."

Maia frowned, glancing at Loki, then back at Lia.

"Anyway, your friend here fucked him up," Maia crowed. "He messed him up *bad*. He'll be even stupider now."

"Maia!" Lia laughed, still wiping her face. "Watch your mouth!"

"Seriously?" Maia gave her a disbelieving look. "You know where I've been living, right?"

Lia sighed, acknowledging that with a frown.

She didn't want to know what Maia had been exposed to over the past five years.

"So?" Maia said, nudging Lia with a hand. "Is this guy your boyfriend? Or what?"

Looking away from where he'd been peering out the passenger-side window at the sky, Loki laughed, then grinned at the two of them.

Before Lia could figure out how to answer that particular question, the God of Mischief turned in his seat, facing Maia directly where she perched between them.

"Yes," he said, adamant. "Yes, my little elf's tiny, tiny sibling... I am her boyfriend. And she is my girlfriend. And my squeeze. And my hunny-bunny. And my little potato."

Maia laughed.

"He's totally nuts, isn't he?" she said, turning to Lia. "Wherever did you find him?"

Again, Loki answered before Lia could speak.

"In the mountains of Nepal," the god said loftily, grinning as Lia bumped up a gear, taking them up the driveway even faster, nearing the Pacific Coast Highway. "She plucked a very valuable ring *right off my finger.* Without my noticing for full *seconds*..."

"She's sneaky like that," Maia acknowledged.

Loki glanced back at her, quirking an eyebrow.

"Sneaky? It is utterly, utterly *unheard* of, my dear, for a human to steal from me. It is utterly *unfathomable,* verging on illegal... possibly full-blown *unnatural.* She did it without me feeling her there until she had already made it several blocks away. She nearly evaded me totally, if I were to be excruciatingly honest... which would have been *most* humiliating. I cannot tell you how long it has been since someone did anything remotely like that to me. I say 'I cannot tell you' in all truthfulness, too, my little raspberry crumpet with cheese filling... because I honestly do not know. Possibly a millennium ago. Possibly never."

Maia let out a delighted laugh, clapping her hands.

Still grinning at her, Loki added,

"I was intrigued and furious. I was shocked and yet single-mindedly *determined* to track down this talented little elf-thief. It is damned lucky I was in Nepal, or it may have taken me *months* to find her, without the aid of supernatural means, given that I am sadly bereft of any notable prescient talents of my own. I confess, I nearly lost her even with that advantage. But then, I really didn't anticipate my little pickpocket hopping on an international flight so quickly."

Turning, he smiled at Lia fondly, tugging on her blond hair.

"Fortunately, a local Buddhist monk, a man they call an *oracle,* tipped me off about the airport," he added to Maia, still caressing Lia's hair. "That was after I paid him money to use his psychic abilities to help me track her down. It is quite lucky I did that right away, too, and didn't get a sandwich first, like I'd contemplated. I barely got to the airport in time."

Maia laughed again, the sound bubbling out of her.

Lia turned to look at him, frowning.

She couldn't stare at him long.

Her hands gripped the steering wheel, rotating it to the right without taking her foot off the gas as she swerved them out onto the highway. She corrected their trajectory at once, bringing them back into the proper lane and gunning it to send the speedometer higher.

"You're joking," Lia retorted, once she had them on the straightaway.

Loki shook his head, grinning wider.

"Not at all, my little lion monkey. My little jam-covered hush-puppy, my little piece of fried spam..."

Maia snort-laughed, looking at Lia.

"Is anything he just said true?" she demanded.

"I love that you're driving so fast," Loki told Lia, winking at her. "My little elf is a talented getaway driver, in addition to all of her other wonderful and highly-intriguing qualities. So many lovely surprises—"

"What is that?" Maia said, pointing between them at something visible through the windshield. "There! Over the water."

Loki turned sharply.

Lowering his head, he stared out the Bugatti's tinted windows.

Lia glanced over as she eased the car around a tighter corner along the cliffside highway, squinting up at the blue sky dotted by white clouds. She saw Loki frown, his gaze narrow, right before she returned her attention to the road, correcting the Bugatti's trajectory as she floored it yet again.

"What is it?" she said, glancing at Loki.

"My brother."

Lia looked over at him, alarmed. "Really?"

"Yes." Loki exhaled, sounding more annoyed than anything. "Clearly, he's caught up with us. I *knew* I felt him there. I dilly-dallied too long inside that fox's den."

"Yes, you did. Why *were* you gone so long inside Gregor's?" Lia demanded. "You scared the hell out of me. I went inside, thinking you were both captured or dead. That couldn't have all been Ernie. Or even the guard who shot at you."

At Loki's silence, Lia smacked his arm, the fingers of her other hand still gripping the steering wheel.

"What happened?"

"Well, it took him a while to deal with that guy, Aston—" Maia began.

"Hush, hush." Loki gave the younger Winchester a faintly warning look, focusing back on Lia. "She doesn't need to know all of that."

Lia felt her alarm spike. "I don't? Who's Aston?"

"I had to attend to a few problems inside," the god said, adjusting his leather coat against the Bugatti's seat. "Unfortunately, it took a bit longer than I'd anticipated. One of those idiots caught me looking around the place before I found your sister. Before I'd quite caught up to him, he called your ex-employer and let him know that something untoward was happening inside his little beachside cottage... which is likely why Gregor and the others rushed back. And likely why the guards came looking for me later."

"Guards?" Lia said, alarmed. "I thought it was *one* guard?"

Loki gave Lia a charming smile.

Lia scowled. "And what happened to that other one? The one who caught you skulking around Gregor's place? Did he shoot you, too?"

"Oh, no. I chucked him over the balcony. It seemed the most efficient thing."

Maia burst out in a laugh.

Lia winced, staring at him. "And what about that guy, Aston?" she said, frowning, glancing back at her sister. "What Maia said? Just now? Or is that the same guy?"

"No, no. An entirely different matter, my dear."

"So what happened to him?" Lia pressed. "Aston?"

Loki gestured fluidly with both hands. "Well, my darling dearest elf, that was an issue I simply *had* to address. You can't possibly fault me for that! Clearly, he lacked a strong father figure in his life, so I had to fill that gap as best I could. In the limited time I had, anyway."

Maia giggled.

Lia snorted, and Loki flashed her another of his wicked smiles.

"One might even say I was fulfilling my *civic duty*," he said loftily. "As a fellow denizen of Earth."

"Are you a denizen of Earth?" Lia said, arching an eyebrow.

"I am *now*. My girlfriend lives here." Loki grinned at her. "Which means all attendant duties are now relevant. Even if I *am* an immigrant."

Maia burst out in another barking laugh.

Lia's kid sister was obviously far too delighted by Loki, and by the way the god chose to explain all of this.

Lia frowned at both of them.

"Okay. So I'm *really* going to need to hear the rest of this story at some point," she said, glancing at the road only to glare at them both a second time. "You get that, right? Like, there's no possible way one or both of you *isn't* telling me every single detail."

Loki was still staring out the window, though, a frown hardening his mouth.

"We might need to go a bit faster, love," he murmured, still following whatever he'd seen with his eyes as it traversed across the sky. "I suspect we'll need to switch cars again soon, too. Likely *very* soon. As in, whenever we get somewhere that might allow us to ditch this one."

Lia fought to think.

She didn't know exactly what was after them, or what Loki feared might happen if his brothers caught up to them, but she had to assume it was bad. Even if it was only bad for Loki himself, that was bad for her, for multiple reasons, and not only because she owed him for getting her sister out of that mafia stronghold in Malibu.

She tried to scan through options objectively.

Clearly, they had to get out of Los Angeles, and soon.

Unseen, if at all possible, since Gregor and now Loki's "hysterical" brother would be tracking them, assuming they weren't following them already.

Lia thought about different ways out of the city.

She considered Burbank Airport, or even flipping around to use the one in Ventura, or Santa Barbara. Conversely, she considered just getting on the freeway and driving for San Diego. Or Las Vegas. Or Palm Springs. Or possibly even going the opposite direction and heading for San Jose, Sacramento, or Fresno, which were far less obvious choices.

She wondered if it would be more or less obvious to simply go back to LAX, maybe catch a plane for Europe.

They could even do the usual thing if they managed to switch out cars.

Meaning, they could just hit the road and drive for the Mexican border.

When she glanced at Loki that time, the god was looking at her.

From his eyes, she found herself thinking he'd heard her thoughts, and that he was mulling through the options she'd presented him with.

"What about a boat?" he said, studying her face as she

looked between him and the view of the road through the windshield.

"Why a boat?" Lia said, pursing her lips.

He grinned faintly, shrugging.

"I like boats."

"Does your brother know that?"

"Sadly, yes." Loki exhaled in a sigh. "I am not sure whether it would occur to him in this scenario or not... but he is aware of my fondness for the sea."

"What do you hate?" Maia asked from the back seat. "What form of transportation do you completely loath? That your brother would also know about?"

Loki looked back at her.

Then he faced forward, tapping his lip with one finger, as if thinking.

"I dislike camels mightily," he said after a beat. "Although they can be amusing. They are such disagreeable creatures. They stink. They are also wont to bite and spit for almost no reason whatsoever. I had one kick me once. Right in the knee."

He pointed down at his knee.

Maia burst out in a laugh. "What else? I don't think we have a lot of camels around here. Maybe at the zoo, but I don't think they'll let us take them for a spin."

When Lia snorted, glancing at her sister in the rearview mirror, Maia grinned at her.

"Anyway," the younger Winchester added. "A camel would *not* be a very sneaky way out of town. They're kinda conspicuous in L.A. On the freeway, especially."

Lia snorted again, rolling her eyes when Maia grinned at her.

"You are *not* helping," she informed her younger sister.

Loki still appeared to be thinking about Maia's question, however.

"Ugh," he said after another pause, grimacing. "I deeply detest buses. Does this mean we have to take a *bus* somewhere? Gross."

Lia burst out in a laugh, unable to help it.

That time, she laughed until her stomach hurt, in spite of the fact that they might have a *god* on their tail shortly, one that could possibly incinerate them with lightning, or pound them with hammers, assuming anything in those myths was remotely true.

"What about a fishing boat?" she teased. "Or maybe we can hitch a ride on an eighteen-wheeler? In the back of a refrigerated car?"

"I would prefer *any* of those things to a bus, my darling girl," Loki sniffed.

He was back to staring out the window, but it seemed to Lia he was using the side mirror more than he was looking directly at whatever he still tracked with his eyes.

"Did Thor go to Gregor's?" Lia asked.

"It appears that way," Loki muttered. "I left a kind of glamour behind for him, hoping to lead him there. I infused a lot of my presence in that thing I left in the living room."

"So, he'll figure out soon that you tricked him," Lia said.

"Yes. It must be assumed so," Loki replied, still watching the side mirror, presumably looking in the direction he'd last seen his brother.

"What the heck was he riding in?" Maia asked from behind their seats. "Was he on a glider? Wearing some kind of jetpack?"

Loki gave her a bare, half-attentive look.

"Unfortunately, no," he said grimly, frowning harder as he stared at the mirror. "The myths about my brother, Thor, having the ability to fly are, thankfully, only myths... likely stemming from our ability to jump dimensions between worlds. Sadly, the myths about my *other* brother, Tyr, being able to fly, are *not* inaccurate. So it's also possible the myths about Thor simply documented the wrong brother..."

From behind the front seats, Maia choked on a laugh.

"Wait... what?"

"You can jump dimensions?" Lia said, ignoring her sister for now. "Can you do that with us? Or just do it yourself, and meet us somewhere later? So your brothers don't catch you?"

"Sadly, no." Loki let out a sigh, his eyes returning to the Bugatti's darkened windows. "Not without my father, Odin, knowing about it. He is attuned to the Bifrost, you see. He would be there, waiting, when I reached the other side... thus, the problem I encountered before. With the Asgardian jail. With the finger wagging, and the blah-blah-blah. It's all most inconvenient. Especially now that I have a human girl-friend, and would very much like to stay here."

He turned his head, looking at Lia grimly.

"While on Earth, I must adhere to the physical rules of Earth."

Lia frowned. "But Tyr can fly?"

"Still a physical phenomenon." Loki shrugged. "Birds fly. Airplanes fly."

Lia's frown deepened at that, but she didn't argue.

"What about the mind-reading?" she said. Worry colored her voice, even as she focused most of her attention on the road. "Can either of your brothers read minds? Can they 'glamour' or whatever, too?"

Loki shook his head.

"No, darling. We each have separate skill sets. For good and for bad. There is a form of mind-reading *all* gods can do, one that requires a connection to be present, something personal. Thankfully, all of us gods have the ability to *block* those connections when we so choose... but we can speak to one another mentally when we don't. I am told Thor can speak to his new wife in this way, as well, even though she is human... in part because they share a past-life bond of some kind."

"Wait... WHAT?" Maia said from the back seat, louder.

Both Lia and Loki ignored her.

"So outline what they *can* do," Lia insisted. "Tyr and Thor. I want to know what we're dealing with. How do you know they're working together? Why wouldn't you just assume it was *Tyr* heading for Gregor's beach house? What makes you so sure Thor is with him?"

Loki pointed out the window.

"Because of that, my little elf."

Lia squinted through the window, following his finger.

Once she did, she saw bolts of blue-white lightning coursing through the large cumulous clouds collecting over the ocean. It struck her in the same set of seconds that she didn't remember seeing clouds like that when they were making the drive from Santa Monica to Malibu in the other direction.

"Shit," she muttered.

"Precisely," Loki said, exhaling another sigh of annoyance. "Anyway, this kind of overt attempt to 'get' me isn't really Tyr's style. Tyr does things differently. He's by far the cleverest of us, although he tries very hard to hide it. I suspect Thor brought him in when I didn't show up at the airport... or we likely would have found Tyr waiting for us at the underbelly of the plane, tapping his foot and annoyed it took us so long. He is rather intuitive like that."

"Oh," Lia said.

She tried to remember if she'd heard any kind of myths about Tyr, but she was coming up blank.

"Yes," Loki sighed, clearly hearing her. "Tyr has also been smart enough to side-step most of the mythologizing around our kind. He's managed to operate mostly off the radar of human beings, and even most of the gods. I used to mock him for that, when we were younger... for the scarce number of temples and altars in his name, the few stories told about him in the old books. He never cared. Tyr is like that monk I paid in Nepal to find you. You cannot appeal to his ego, or even his wallet, despite his bizarre habit of collecting gold trinkets and squirreling them away. Oh, except that he kills people. And he can fly."

"He sounds... like he could be a problem," Lia admitted.

"He invariably is, once he decides to get involved." Loki sighed again, folding his arms across his chest. "Thankfully, that's not as often as Thor would probably like."

Loki aimed his gaze back out the window, focusing on the side mirror as he looked back up the coast of Malibu.

"I wonder what dear brother Thor used to coax him into getting involved *this* time," he grumbled. "I don't think I've done anything to annoy Tyr lately. I generally go out of my way to *not* annoy him."

Sniffing, Loki shrugged, refolding his arms. "I did hear Tyr took a liking to Thor's new wife. Perhaps *she* asked him to get involved. If only to appease her boor of a husband."

Lia felt her jaw clench.

Loki still hadn't given her that list of things each of his brothers could do, in terms of supernatural powers, but she felt like she had the gist of it.

Thor could make clouds, thunder... and, more to the point, lightning.

Tyr could fly, eccentrically collected gold, and "killed people," whatever that meant.

"He can also read minds," Loki said, glancing at her. "Tyr. But he must be physically close to the person. He must be able to *see* them, I believe. And he can only do so on some worlds, not on all of them. I can't remember if he can do this on Earth or not..."

Loki tapped his full lips with a finger, thinking.

"...I believe he *cannot* do it here. But I don't remember, honestly. I haven't been in this world at the same time as Tyr in probably a thousand of your years."

Lia nodded, remembering Maia enough to glance at her sister in the rearview mirror.

Seeing the blankly incredulous look on her baby sister's face, Lia opened her mouth to say something... when a flash lit up her view in the rearview mirror, jerking her eyes to the side and behind her sister's blond head.

A huge fireball was rising on the coast.

Lia gasped, and Maia turned her head, staring out the back window at the rising mushroom cloud.

"Ah," Loki said, following their gazes. "I suspected Thor might not like Gregor all that much. I left him a note in that mirage about who your employer truly was. And what his 'business' consists of. And what his henchmen like to do to human cubs."

When Lia glanced back at the road, then over at Loki, the god was frowning, his arms crossed even more tightly across his chest.

"Are we in trouble?" she asked him.

He looked over at her, his green eyes flat, but clearly conveying his answer.

Nodding, Lia bit her lip.

They were just coming into Santa Monica.

12

TRADING IN THE CAR

"Leave it," Loki urged, motioning towards Lia's hand holding the Bugatti's keys. "We must go. It's likely they are tracking the car. We must put as much distance between it and us as we can."

"The car?" Lia blinked at him. "How would they be tracking the car?"

"My brother Tyr would have questioned Gregor and his people about this. They will look for the car first, since I am doing what I can to block their efforts at tracking me."

Pausing, Loki added,

"And Thor may not be as clever as Tyr, but he is also no fool. For months now, he has been using various cameras around the human world to try and find me... and even to track and follow the ring itself. It is part of the reason you encountered me in a part of the world where you did. Those cameras are far less common in that part of Asia. I've been doing my best to 'stay off the grid,' as you humans put it. I had hoped Thor might eventually get bored of pursuing me and go back to California to play footsie with his new wife."

Lia frowned, glancing up at the CCTV cameras she could

see even now, on the street where they currently stood, directly across from Venice Beach.

Police cameras lived at the traffic lights and at various intervals down the block, but that was only part of it. There was also the camera in the ATM machine near the bank, the security cameras at the gas station and outside the jewelry store on the west side of the street—

"Yes, yes, I know," Loki said, impatient.

"So they're watching us right now?" Lia said, swallowing.

"Unlikely," the god told her. "But there is a good chance they will find us that way eventually. We have some time before they would resort to such things, versus looking for the car themselves. But we must get some distance. In addition to the problem with the cameras, the closer we brothers are to one another, the more we can feel one another—"

"*Feel* one another?" Lia paled, hearing the faint panic in her voice. "Can you feel them now? Right now?"

Loki nodded to her grimly.

"Yes. I can feel both of them. My brother Thor, especially. He has a tendency to... project his feelings, I guess you could say. Rather vehemently."

When Lia glanced up at the sky, half-expecting to get struck by lightning, or perhaps hit in the head with a silver hammer, Loki motioned to her sharply, his words urgent.

"Come, little elf, come. We can still outrun them, but we must be quick."

His words snapped her back to the present.

She knew how to run.

She'd done it plenty of times before.

Throwing her satchel's strap over her neck and head, Lia tossed the Bugatti's keys through the partly-opened window so that they landed on the front seat. She gripped the satchel in one hand to keep it from bouncing too hard against her hip, and took Loki's offered hand. Speeding her walk to a near-jog to match Loki's long steps, she glanced over her shoulder to make sure Maia followed closely behind.

Her sister walked fast, staying right behind both of them.

Even so, Maia looked dazed, like she wasn't quite sure what was happening.

Lia wondered if the reality of having run away from Gregor was finally sinking in for her baby sister, because it was sinking in for Lia.

Had she lost her mind?

Gregor had contacts all over the world.

He wasn't even the head honcho at the Syndicate, and all of the money she owed Gregor eventually trickled up to them. Hell, the Syndicate didn't even operate primarily out of the United States, much less Los Angeles. Lia wasn't sure *where* it was based out of exactly, but she'd always assumed somewhere in Eastern Europe.

Whatever the truth of who or what ran the highest echelons of the Syndicate, it was bigger than Lia could really fathom. Only one thing struck her as absolutely true: there was no distance far enough they could go to get away from the Syndicate and its people.

The Syndicate had operatives in probably half of the major cities of the world.

Possibly more than that.

Possibly all of them.

Even if Gregor was dead, there was a damned good chance the Syndicate would still come after her and Maia, and possibly Loki now, as well.

They might even come after them harder.

And that was in *addition* to all the insanity with flying gods, mystical lightning storms, and whatever else Loki was concerned about.

Glancing at Maia a second time, Lia frowned, still half-jogging beside Loki.

Come to think of it, Gregor might not be on Maia's mind at all.

Maia might be reacting more to the conversation they'd had in the Bugatti on the way down here. Maybe she'd decided that her big sister, Lia, had gone nuts, and her big sister's new "friend" was *also* batshit crazy, and likely to get both of them killed.

Lia couldn't exactly blame her for that.

"This way," Loki urged, pulling her down a side street.

Lia didn't know Venice all that well. Still, she started to think she might know where they were going when Loki took them down a few more streets. That suspicion was confirmed when they rounded a last, multi-story building, and Lia saw the harbor ahead.

"Won't they look for us on a boat?" Lia said, frowning, still half-running at his side as they headed for Marina del Rey. "You said Thor knew you well enough to look for you on a boat. It was the first thing you said."

"Come, come, little elf. Better for us to get out of here now, than for us to get bogged down in details. There are boats here. We are here. We mustn't be choosy."

When Lia gave him a skeptical look, Loki squeezed her fingers.

"Don't worry," he added. "I planned ahead."

Holding up a set of keys with a yellow flotation device attached, he jangled them.

"I don't intend to wander around the docks, willy-nilly," he said. "Or even to steal some poor slob's boat and leave him stranded like we did with the car. We have a ride."

Lia stared at the keys incredulously.

"Where on *Earth* did you get those?"

"I found them. At the mobster's place. They were just sitting there... on a hook... in his study... behind a locked door. Along with a photo of the boat. And a few guns."

Loki produced a handgun from his brown, leather coat, showing her that, as well.

Lia laughed, unable to help it.

"You are unbelievable," she smiled, kissing his cheek.

"And resourceful," he smiled back. "Right? Your snuggle-bunny is resourceful?"

She couldn't exactly disagree with that.

Loki led her down to the docks, somehow getting them past a locked gate, then walking them onto the main pier. He told Lia roughly what they were looking for, and both of them scanned the boats on either side, looking for Gregor's.

Walking down the center pier, Lia focused on one side of the dock and Loki the other. After maybe five minutes where they'd passed probably half the boats in the marina, Loki squeezed her hand, jerking his head to their right.

Without waiting, he began leading her down one of the side piers to a large yacht tied at the end.

"Is that it?" Lia said, doubtful as she squinted at the white boat. "Are you sure?"

"That is the one, precious. I saw the photo, remember?"

Nodding, Lia followed him to the end of the dock. She hesitated while Loki boarded in front of her, looking for a name on the side of the boat while the god climbed up the side and jumped down, heading immediately for the ship's bow.

Lia found the letters on the edge then, in black paint.

"Mona Lisa Surprise," Lia read, frowning.

Their mother was Lisa.

Lia remembered Gregor calling her his "Mona Lisa," back when they were dating.

Grunting a little, Lia shrugged, looking away from the cursive script.

"Surprise, asshole," she muttered, grabbing the silver

guardrails and yanking herself up the ladder leading to the main deck.

When Maia grabbed the silver guardrails behind her, about to follow Lia onto the boat, Loki called down, raising his voice.

"Maia, love? Be a dear and get those, would you?"

He pointed to the ropes tying the yacht to their piece of pier.

Lia looked back from where she'd reached the ship's deck, watching as her sister obligingly climbed back down and began untying ropes, throwing each one up once she'd pried the fitted nooses off the wooden posts.

Whatever doubts Maia might have about Loki and Lia, she seemed to shake at least some of it off as she made her way around the ship, preparing them to leave.

Lia waited for her, watching Maia untie the last rope before she walked back around the full length of the boat. Returning to the same ladder Lia used, Maia grabbed the silver guardrails and climbed up to join them, scaling the ridged metal steps rapidly and yanking herself up with her arms. Lia offered her hand when her sister got to the top, and Maia took it, letting Lia pull her the rest of the way onto the main deck.

When she reached the top, Maia hugged her.

Lia hugged her back, closing her eyes.

She hoped like hell Loki was right, that his escape plan would work.

She couldn't bear it if someone took Maia away from her again.

Even as she thought it, Maia pulled out of the hug, grinning at her.

"Did you see the Jetskis?" she said, pointing to the stern of the ship. "AWESOME, right? There's three of them, too, so we can all go out together!"

Before Lia could answer, her little sister turned her blond head towards Loki, who was climbing the stairs up to the cockpit at the front of the boat.

"Where are we off to now, Loki, God of Mischief?" Maia called out, a faint smirk visible at the edges of her mouth. "Somewhere exciting?"

She raised a hand to shield her eyes from the sun, still watching Loki as he unlocked and entered the enclosed cockpit high above the main deck. When Maia began walking towards him, Lia went with her, glancing back over her shoulder at the pier, looking for anyone who might be watching them, or in the process of calling the police about a stolen yacht.

She followed Maia all the way up the stairs to the glass-enclosed compartment.

By then, Loki was already behind the round wheel, having started the boat's engine using Gregor's keys.

Lia looked around as the engine roared to life, noting all the gauges and screens and maps. She watched as Loki began to spin the wheel, his hand on the throttle as he eased them backwards out of the docking space.

"Well?" Maia said, as Loki spun the wheel again, and the yacht began moving forward. "Are you going to answer me? Or is that going to be some kind of weird surprise? Like you're taking us to Atlantis? Or one of the weird places in Jason of the Argonauts?"

Loki rolled his eyes, looking at Lia.

"This girl needs a serious education, my love. She's got her mythologies all hopelessly mixed up. I can hardly be expected to check them for accuracy when she's off by a few thousand years in either direction... or when she has the *entirely wrong* part of the globe."

Maia laughed, nudging his arm.

Something about her sister's easy affection with Loki made Lia smile.

"Where are we going?" Maia insisted. "Tell me!"

"Why, Mexico, of course." The god smiled at her, taking them out of the marina and aiming the ship for the open water. "Or would you prefer Hawaii?"

Lia snorted, but Maia jumped up and down, clapping her hands.

"Oooooh, Hawaii!" she said, looking at Lia. "Definitely Hawaii! Please? Can we *please* go there? I've always wanted to go!"

Loki laughed.

He glanced at Lia, giving her a wink.

"We might need to get to an airport first, love," he said, his eyes holding a visible heat as he continued to look at Lia, even though he directed his words at Maia. "But we'll ask big sis. See what we can do for you, yes? Asgard knows, I'm helpless in the face of her desires..."

13

BELONGING

L oki taught Maia how to steer the ship.

Then, after giving her a basic tutorial on how to hold the same direction and some of the rules of operating on the open sea, he caught hold of Lia's arm and took her with him to explore the yacht below-deck.

They walked through all of the various compartments and cabins together.

Truthfully, given how quickly Loki had absconded with the boat, Lia was just relieved they found no one sleeping down there, or one of Gregor's goons waiting for them in one of the cabins with a loaded gun.

That being said, they did find some interesting things below deck.

Loki seemed able to sniff out contraband everywhere he went.

He found Gregor's safe under a painting over the master cabin's bed.

Cracking that open—using a method Lia couldn't discern, but that definitely didn't involve the usual safe-cracking methods she knew, or any kind of explosives—the god pulled

out a few stacks of important-looking papers, some cash, and
an enormous bag of what looked to Lia like cocaine, but Loki
informed her was heroin.

Lia worried a bit, watching Loki heft the drugs in his
hand, raising his eyebrows at her suggestively. Then the god
laughed, presumably at whatever look he saw on Lia's face.
Before she could decide how to react, Loki opened one of the
round view ports and tossed the entire bag out the window
and into the Pacific.

Once it sank in what he'd done, Lia threw back her head,
laughing.

"Just a little test, my dear," the god informed her, grinning
as he leaned over to kiss her on the mouth. Pulling away, he
studied her eyes, his lighter green ones holding a faint scrutiny. "I've never been one for such substances. Truthfully, I'm
not even a huge fan of spirits. Although they *are* handy to
have around when my brothers come calling."

Remembering the bottle of Scotch she had in her bag, and
the one she'd seen Loki swig in the back of the taxi, Lia
frowned, but didn't comment. She was more than happy to
donate the aged liquor to getting their butts out of here
clean, if it came to that.

If she could bribe either of Loki's brothers with the
Scotch, it was definitely theirs.

Truthfully, the idea of flying gods who could wield lightning and who had a grudge with her current boyfriend—who
was no picnic, granted, but hardly *evil,* as he pointed out—
still tugged worriedly at the back of her mind.

"Boyfriend," Loki said, grinning at her. "You just called me
your boyfriend."

"I said no such thing," Lia informed him, giving him a
mock lofty look.

"Oh, I heard it," Loki said, tugging on her fingers. *"Very*
clearly."

He leaned over the king-sized bed in the master cabin, kissing her.

He kissed her harder the second time, using his tongue, his fingers curling into and clutching her long hair. When Lia remembered Maia upstairs and started to pull back, Loki smiled at her, kissing her face, then her throat.

"Don't worry, little elf," he murmured. "I won't molest you in front of baby sis."

Sliding off the thick duvet on top of the mattress, he motioned towards the three tall closets built into the wall.

"Speaking of which," he added, walking to the first set of double doors. "You should probably find some clothes to change into, while we're down here. No reason to put on the dirty ones from Nepal, if you can find something that fits you here."

He flung open the first set of doors, frowning as he peered inside.

Moving on to the next set of doors, he opened those, too.

Then he bent down, and began opening drawers.

"I think there are things here you can wear," he said, thoughtfully.

When Lia walked over to join him, Loki stroked her hair back from her face, kissing her mouth again, more sensually that time, then the side of her face.

"You did call me your boyfriend," he murmured, his voice a soft rebuke. "Does that mean you've finally made up your mind about me? I *did* give you loads and loads of extra time, you know. I'd said before you only had until our arrival on this continent to decide."

Lia laughed, pushing lightly at his chest.

"That was a few hours ago," she reminded him, her voice faintly scolding. "Tops. And I haven't exactly had a lot of quiet time to think since we met. It's all explosions and flying brothers and kidnappings and car theft. Not to mention us having to escape from the airplane in the first place to get away from Gregor and his goons…"

She looked up at him, grinning into the god's face.

When she met Loki's gaze, however, the god's expression was deadly serious.

"So you need more time, Lia?" he said. "To know if you belong to me?"

Lia blinked, staring up at him. "What?" She frowned a little. "Are you really giving me an ultimatum? Or some kind of time limit?"

Loki shook his head.

"No," he said, his voice definite. "I am not. I simply need to know where you are now."

She continued to frown up at him, studying his face.

"Where is this coming from?" she said finally. "You must know I'm crazy about you."

"But what does that mean?"

Lia blinked again. "What do you think it means? I *like* you, Loki. I like you a lot. And I trust you enough to risk my life, and more importantly, my sister's life… on risking trying to leave Gregor so we can be together. I trust you enough to believe you and I are in this together, that we can escape the people chasing us *together.* That's more than I've *ever* had. With *anyone,* Loki. Even my own mother—"

"But do you *accept* me, Lia?" he said, those pale, leaf-green eyes studying hers. "I know it's a lot to ask, given who and what I am, but *have* you made up your mind?"

When she frowned, staring up at him, he took one of her hands in both of his, tilting his head as he looked at her.

His voice grew firm, direct.

"Is this simply expediency for you?" he queried. "A way out of a bad situation, yes… but with the clear thought in your mind that it will not last. That you are sure to find a far better situation, once you no longer need me?"

He paused.

"I trust you to tell me the truth," he added, still watching her eyes. "I trust you to *know* the truth about yourself, Lia. To view this realistically. And honestly."

She studied his eyes back, even more bewildered.

"Are you asking whether I see potential with us?" she said, losing the coyness in her voice. "As in, long-term dating, versus a fling of some kind? Because I thought that was pretty obvious. Do I seem like I'm about to run away?"

"Not just dating." Loki shook his head, his eyes going even more still. "I'm looking for a trifle more than your human 'dating,' my elf."

"Like what?" Lia said, still more puzzled than anything.

Loki looked away.

She saw his eyes grow briefly pained as he gazed out the row of viewports at the rolling ocean. Lia saw what might have been indecision on his face, right before he looked at her again, his gaze even more intense than before.

"I feel we belong together," he said simply.

There was a silence.

"You mean as partners?" Lia said, still trying to understand. "Like what you said on the plane? When you said there was a job you wanted me to do?"

"There is no job, Lia," he said, his voice a touch sharper.

For a few seconds they only looked at one another.

Staring up at those pale green, faintly glowing eyes, Lia felt almost dizzy.

Then, even as she felt she was being tested somehow, and somehow failing, without even knowing what the test was about—her mind clicked into a sharper focus.

What he was asking her felt simple, suddenly.

Simple, and utterly obvious, both in terms of the question and her inevitable answer.

She found herself caressing his jaw, tracing the outline of

his features, watching as he closed his eyes, noting how long his dark lashes were. She ran her fingers lightly over his jaw, his throat, the back of his neck, tracing the lines of muscle leading down to the band of gold and black letters over the top of his chest.

"I'll only leave when you make me, Loki," she said, soft.

She felt Loki react.

He flinched, but it was more than that.

The green eyes opened, and he was staring at her again, his gaze full, his jaw tight. He leaned down, kissing her tenderly, and something about the kiss caught her breath, making her clutch at his shirt. A few seconds later, he raised his head, looking at her, then he kissed her again, laying his fingers and hands on the middle part of her chest, just above her solar plexus.

Something about the placement felt exceedingly deliberate.

She swore she heard him murmur something when he kissed her the next time, words in that other language she'd heard him speak a few times before.

As he did, an electric-feeling pulse slid through her, from his fingers to the center of her chest. Whatever it was, it had emotion wrapped into it, a kind of heartbreaking intensity and want that clutched at her chest, making her gasp.

She reached up, gripping his hand where he'd pressed his palm against her.

When she looked up, he met her gaze.

His eyes were glowing.

They glowed like nothing she'd ever seen before, even with him.

She stared at that otherworldly light, mesmerized. She'd never seen it that bright before. She'd never seen so much behind the lights in his eyes before, either, but unlike the times before, she couldn't quite read the emotion that stood out in those pale irises, either.

Whatever it was, it struck Lia as complex, as utterly guileless, as intense to the point of being difficult to look at.

Something about it also struck her as borderline vulnerable.

Maybe just the fact that he let her see it was a kind of vulnerability.

He left his hand there, in the middle of her chest.

His fingers seemed to grow hotter as he did, the electric current more filled with charge, more intense, more filled with that emotion, until Lia was fighting to breathe.

When Loki finally took his hand away, his eyes were glowing like searchlights.

He smiled at her, and she fell into that smile, lost in those light-filled eyes.

"I had better go up and check on baby sis," he said gently.

Leaning down, he kissed her face, stroking her cheek with his fingertips.

Then he stepped back, removing himself from her immediate space, disorienting Lia even more when he suddenly felt too far away.

"Take a shower if you like, love," he said, caressing her jaw tenderly with the same hand.

Lia closed her eyes, leaning into his touch.

Loki's words and fingers grew lulling, seeming to pull her deeper into him.

"Come upstairs whenever you're ready."

He kissed her again, smiling down at her, and she saw that intensity of feeling there sharpen, the raw emotion hitting at her, catching in her chest. The light in his green irises was slowly beginning to fade, but the emotion didn't dim along with it.

"I won't let us crash into the shore," he promised softly,

kissing her again. "Or into another boat. Or into either of my brothers, for that matter..."

He began slowly backing away.

Lia watched him leave, feeling almost in a trance.

She jumped a little, startled when he turned at the last minute, and began to walk out of the main cabin briskly. Within seconds, the God of Mischief disappeared entirely from her view, shutting the cabin door behind him without a backwards glance.

Lia stood there for a few seconds, unmoving.

She felt bewildered at first.

Then she almost felt sad.

Well... not sad exactly.

Maybe more worried. Disappointed?

Whatever the exact emotion was, she couldn't determine the source at first. Then she realized a part of her was startled, maybe more like disappointed, that Loki had left so quickly, given what he'd just told her to do. The god had given her privacy, rather than watch her get naked, offer or ask for oral sex, or just have his hands all over her in the period before Lia got into the shower.

She wasn't truly disappointed he hadn't done it... not exactly... but she wasn't exactly *relieved* he hadn't done it, either.

She did wonder if something about Maia being here had cooled his interest in her on that front. Maybe he saw her more maternally now.

Maybe he saw her as more of a friend.

But that didn't make sense, either.

If he was cooling on the sex front with her, then what had all of that been about asking Lia what she wanted? Trying to determine if she wanted to be his girlfriend? Pushing her to give him some kind of answer, even though answering him now made no logical sense?

She barely knew him.

Loki barely knew her.

Turning all of it over in her head, Lia frowned, shouldering the leather coat off her arms and letting it fall to the floor.

Maybe hoping to distract herself, she walked over to explore the various closets and drawers, just as Loki had done a few minutes earlier. She thought maybe if she focused on something normal, something mundane, something concrete, it might clear her head.

Maybe it would even allow her to think about Loki objectively for once.

She opened every single closet, cupboard, and drawer.

Loki had been right.

She found jeans that looked like they would fit, along with cotton pants, both the straight-legged and the stretchy kind. She also found skirts of various lengths, along with a stack of shorts, sweat pants, T-shirts, nylon vests for when it was cold, a few jackets and windbreakers, and at least six pairs of tennis shoes, all of them roughly a size too big.

Gregor obviously provisioned the place for at least one female guest.

He must have a girlfriend roughly Lia's size and height.

Just with bigger feet.

In the end, Lia grabbed a pair of loose black shorts, a violet, spandex tank-top in lieu of a bra, since none of the bras she found would remotely fit her, and a faded-pink, scoop-necked sweatshirt with the words "Sailor Baby" on the front, just because some part of her found the caption amusing.

Once she'd settled on a pile of clean clothes, including socks and the smallest-looking pair of tennis shoes she could find, Lia walked around the perimeter of the cabin, trying doors again, looking for the shower.

Within minutes, she found that, too.

Setting the clean clothes on the king-sized bed, she peeled the skin-tight white dress off her body with a sigh. After a few seconds' back and forth, she chucked the dress out the round view port, like Loki had with the bag of heroin.

The thing was trashed.

Even so, some part of her felt a faint regret, watching it go.

Sighing a bit, she walked, fully nude, to the cabin's shower.

14

NEVER TRUST A TRICKSTER GOD

Lia was still in the shower when the lights flickered.

She paused, looking up, soap and shampoo suds running down her back. She held her breath, but the lights stayed on, glowing faintly from the round fixtures above her.

She went back to rinsing off—

When the lights flickered again, longer that time.

Lia looked up and around, still wiping suds off her forehead and hair. She glanced around at the Fiberglas shower cubicle, worried there might be an electrical problem in the bathroom itself, possibly in one of the light fixtures—

When the lights cut out entirely.

Lia blinked, feeling her heart start to pound in her chest.

It wasn't pitch black where she was, at least. One of those round viewports lived in the bulkhead just outside the shower door, so Lia could see reasonably well from the afternoon sunlight, even inside the translucent shower cubicle.

A shiver of foreboding went through her anyway.

After a pause where she waited to see if the lights would come back on, she quickly finished rinsing the last of the soap and conditioner out of her hair, then spent a few more seconds rinsing her body off under the shower head.

Twisting the silver shower valve to turn off the water, she flung open the door and jumped out, snatching the nearest full-sized towel off the room's one rack. Rubbing it all over her body quickly, she used it to soak up some of the excess water in her hair, then tossed it onto the bathroom floor.

Feeling her heart thud louder in her chest, she opened the door to the master quarters.

She didn't enter all at once.

Peering inside, she saw no one, heard nothing, and let out a half-exhale of relief.

After a faint pause where she looked and listened a few seconds longer, Lia left the bathroom totally, re-entering the cabin and looking around in the gloomy light, her hair still dripping down her back.

The power was clearly off in here, too.

Like with the shower cubicle, sunlight shone through the row of viewports on either side, filling the captain's quarters with afternoon sun. Even so, Lia remembered leaving the overhead lights on in here. She could also see the digital clock was dead, and so was the electronic thermostat.

She grabbed the pile of clothes she'd pulled together prior to her shower.

Still staring around, she threw them on as fast as she could.

Once she got on the black shorts, the violet tank top and pink sweatshirt, she sat on the bed, yanking on the low ankle socks she'd found, and then the oversized tennis shoes, tying them up quickly as she felt her heart pounding harder in her chest.

Why hadn't Loki come down to tell her what was going on?

Why hadn't Maia?

Only then did she realize the engine had stopped, too.

Cursing under her breath, Lia ran for the cabin door, yanking it open and taking the stairs on the other side as fast as she could. Using the guardrails on either side, she propelled herself faster as she yanked her body up the narrow passage.

She made it up to the main deck and half-ran to the front of the ship, where the enclosed cockpit lived. Lia made it to the base of the Fiberglas stairs that led up to the navigation area, and came to a dead stop, staring up at the sky.

Something was coming towards them.

Something was *definitely* coming towards them.

It was coming really, really fast.

Whatever that something was, it sparked blue and white electrical charges out like a halo around a dark patch in the middle, like some kind of supernatural comet. It didn't appear to be slowing, the closer it got.

Lia felt her breath stop when she realized it looked more like it was about to slam right into them... right before exploding the ship in a mushroom cloud of blue-white flames.

Remembering what she'd seen of Gregor's house from the Bugatti, Lia felt all the air leave her lungs, even as the blood drained from her face.

She got the air back first.

She sucked in a chest-full, then immediately let it out.

"LOKI!" she screamed up the stairs. "LOKI! WHAT DO WE DO?"

There was no answer.

Biting her lip, Lia began taking the stairs two at a time up to the cockpit.

She reached the top deck, and ran into the small room, past the open door, which was swinging and banging lazily into the outer wall.

"LOKI!"

She came to a dead stop, staring around the inside of the navigation area.

Someone had tied a rope around the steering wheel, locking it in place.

All the instruments looked dead.

The engine was definitely dead.

No Loki.

No Maia.

Feeling her heart leap to her throat, even as her breath caught in her chest, she searched every corner of the small cockpit, then ran for the door and half-fell, half-ran down the Fiberglas steps. The door continued to bang into the wall from the rocking motion of the stalled ship, but Lia ran by it, barely noticing.

She looked over her shoulder as she ran, staring up at the sky, tracking the progress of the approaching object, feeling the air hitching and locking inside her lungs.

"LOKI!" she screamed, running across the main deck of the ship. "WHERE ARE YOU? WHERE DID YOU TAKE MY SISTER, YOU PIECE OF SHIT? WHERE *ARE* YOU?"

She ran up and down the length of the yacht before she had to admit to herself they weren't up there. Running for the stairs leading below deck, she looked through the galley and two guest bedrooms below. She dug through the smaller spaces next: a pantry, a general storage area, two "heads," or bathrooms, a small common space.

No Loki. No Maia.

Remembering something, she ran back towards the captain's quarters.

Sliding and stumbling down the narrow staircase, she entered the main cabin and looked around the sunshine-bathed space.

Finally locating what she was looking for, she grabbed her

leather coat off the king-sized bed, going through the pockets frantically until she found the secret compartment she'd had made within the inner seam, the one where she'd hidden Loki's magical ring.

The compartment was empty.

The ring was gone.

No Loki. No sister.

No ring.

Lia cursed loudly, throwing the leather coat at the floor.

Pacing the cabin's plush rug in her oversized tennis shoes, Lia let out a second, louder, more infuriated scream, staring around the wood-paneled cabin, trying to decide what to do, where they could have gone.

She couldn't believe how stupid she'd been, how insanely gullible.

She was still standing there, half-paralyzed by rage, by panicked worry for Maia, by a less-tangible grief mixed with a hotter wanting of revenge—

—when something slammed into the main deck of the ship, making a sound like a building had just landed on top of her.

For a few seconds, Lia Winchester thought she was dead.

She was sure she was dead.

Really, being dead was the only thing that made sense at this point.

Dead or not, she hit the deck.

She dropped in pure instinct, without thought.

She dropped before the impact would have thrown her down by force.

Landing on her hands, toes, and thighs on the plush, pale blue carpet, Lia remained perfectly still, panting as she

listened to the rolling crash of impact and what sounded like
thunder grow louder, then gradually softer overhead.

The entire ship started rocking crazily.

The rocking got worse, growing violent, like it got caught
in the wake of a gargantuan boat, or maybe the wash of a
giant sea-creature.

It was nearly enough to make Lia sick.

Somewhere in that, maybe in her effort not to lose her
lunch, she lost her ability to grip the carpet and rolled sideways, crashing into the bulkhead to her right, and knocking
open a storage cabinet built into the wood-paneled walls.

The ship rocked back the other way, and fishing rods,
wire, hand-nets, and bobbers rained down on her, along with
a few storage containers, seashells, and other knick-knacks.
The bigger, heavier pieces made her gasp and throw up her
arms, protecting her head.

She managed to crawl sideways and then to another
segment of wall, where she gripped the edge of a built-in
bench covered in cushions that had to be Velcro-ed onto the
wood. Gripping the edge of the bench, she pulled herself
carefully to her feet, and lurched and swayed her way to the
door leading to the staircase and the upper deck.

Her hand on the handle, she stood there, panting,
wondering if she should open it.

She already knew who was on the main deck of the ship—
assuming she wasn't completely crazy, or Loki was a much
better liar than she thought.

It had to be Loki's brothers.

Given what they must think of her, should she really go
up there? Or should she hide from them? Maybe in the
pantry on the other side of the galley? Or in the far back of
the dry storage? Or maybe even in the shower cubicle she'd
just used?

Remembering then, what these people may have done to

Gregor's house in Malibu, she clenched her jaw.

She couldn't risk them blowing up the boat with her in it.

If she was their captive, at least she could potentially get away.

Maybe they'd even let her go.

Or, better yet, maybe they'd help her find her sister.

Would they really harm her, if she told them Loki stole the ring from her? Right before he kidnapped her kid sister as leverage?

Clenching her jaw, she realized she had no choice.

She needed their help.

She'd never get Maia away from Loki without help from someone.

If she was being honest—and again, assuming she wasn't totally insane—she'd never get Maia away from Loki without help from someone supernatural.

She'd seen what Loki could do. He could just glamour himself and Maia into palm trees, or mailboxes, or two old Guatamalan cow-herders, and Lia would walk right by them, never recognizing either one.

No, whatever Loki turned out to be, Lia had no illusions about her chances against him.

She couldn't handle him on her own.

She needed to go upstairs, see if whatever was there might be willing and able to handle the Trickster God for her.

Clenching her jaw tighter at the thought, Lia jerked open the door, gripping the sides of the opening once she had it free from the wall.

Slowly, holding each of the two guardrails for dear life, she began to make her way up the steep stairs, aiming her feet for the main deck of the ship. She braced herself with each step, hoping she was ready to face whatever just crashed-landed into the million-dollar yacht she'd helped steal.

If not, Maia might be lost to her forever.

15

GOD-BROTHERS

L ia poked her head out of hole in the deck, pausing from where she'd been ascending the stairs to carefully look around.

At first, all she saw was smoke.

She didn't see any fire.

Strangely, she also didn't feel any heat coming from the area with the thickest concentration of gray and white smoke plumes billowing up.

She was still staring at the smokiest part of the ship's deck, when two forms walked out of the dense air, one of them being probably the largest person Lia had ever seen.

The other one was almost as big, and roughly the same height.

His build made her think more of fighters she'd met, or possibly a professional acrobat. Really, he looked and moved more like some combination of fighter-dancer. With his graceful, predatory tread, Lia found herself thinking if he'd been human, she would have assumed he was some kind of highly-trained martial artist.

Given everything she'd seen and experienced over the

past few days, she found herself thinking he likely *wasn't* human, though.

Raising her hand to shield her eyes and squinting through the smoke, she tried to remember everything Loki had told her about his two brothers.

She looked at the huge one first, the one she actually recognized, even if this was her first time *really* seeing him, versus seeing a mirage.

He definitely looked different now.

That was in spite of how accurately Loki captured his likeness at Gregor's.

Lia focused on his long, thick, reddish-blond hair, the statue-like face that was almost too beautiful to look real, the ice-blue eyes. She glanced over his broad shoulders, the thick chest, and found herself stifling the urge to laugh when she saw how normally he was dressed, especially after how Loki clothed the illusion-version in Malibu.

He wore black slacks, a white, collared shirt, open at the throat, and a suit jacket that had smudges of white and black on it from the smoke. The white shirt also had a few black smudges on the front. So did the pale skin of the giant's neck.

None of it took away from his beauty, though.

If he was a god, apart from the clothes, he was more or less what she would have assumed a god would look like, whether Norse or any other kind.

That had to be Thor.

It had to be.

Lia's eyes turned to the fighter-dancer-martial-artist next.

His dark eyes already stared at her face.

Lia got lost there briefly, in the god's eyes, like something about them pulled her into his very soul, or maybe just outside her own body.

Those near-black irises had a kind of fire burning behind them, despite their dark color. It was as if red embers lived there, inside that deep, coal-black, but strangely, she wasn't afraid of him, or of the light she saw there.

She found him, and his eyes, oddly comforting.

She flinched, blinking when he looked away,

It was like feeling a connection snap.

Then she was watching both of them walk towards her, one moving like a champion weight-lifter or heavyweight boxer, the other like a feral cat.

Swallowing as they approached her directly, she didn't move until they halted, nearly in unison, just past the edge of the stairway where she crouched.

Fighting to keep her expression calm, Lia forced herself to take those last few steps, climbing up onto the wooden deck to stand in front of them.

The yacht was still swaying from the impact of the two gods, but much less violently than before. She could maintain her balance without holding onto anything, but still had her knees slightly bent to absorb the rocking motion.

She swallowed again, looking between those two faces.

The blond one looked angry.

More than angry.

He also looked confused, borderline bewildered as he stared at her.

Lia turned to look at the dark-eyed one again, who had to be Tyr, God of War, and the "cleverest brother," according to Loki, God of Mischief.

Taking in the expression on Tyr's face now, Lia blinked, startled.

She'd expected the expression on Thor's face.

She expected anger, confusion, frustration, a demand for explanations.

She'd expected them both gods to be furious at finding her here instead of Loki.

Maybe for the same reason, Thor's expected rage was a lot

less disorienting than looking into the eyes of Tyr, which held a faint if knowing humor. The God of War's perfect mouth twitched, as if he were holding back a laugh, right before he glanced at Thor, smiling wider when he saw his brother's near-boiling anger.

Something about this situation had definitely hit at Tyr's funny bone.

Lia had no earthly idea what that could possibly be.

Before she'd fully absorbed and made sense of Tyr's humorous near-grin, Thor broke the silence among the three of them, his voice a harsh bark.

"Who, in the name of Asgard, are you?" he snapped, glaring at her with those ice-blue eyes. "And why *in the gods* has my brother marked you as his mate?"

Lia stared up at him, her mouth ajar.

Before she could collect herself enough to attempt to answer, before she could even remotely make sense of Thor's words, Tyr, the God of War standing next to him, burst out in an uncontrollable laugh...

...right before he walked up to Lia, shocking the hell out of her by giving her a warm bear hug, squeezing her to his chest before he kissed her on the cheek.

She was still gaping up at him when the god released her, laughing again.

He shook her lightly by the arms, grinning down at her face.

"Welcome to the family, sister," he said, those embers in his dark irises burning with a merrier twinkle. "You are most, *most* welcome. Despite my brother Thor's lack of manners, we are both very happy to greet you as companion to our rather troublesome brother, Loki... and we wish you all the happiness and good fortune in the world."

Tyr let out another short guffaw, looking delightedly at Thor.

"As our father Odin knows, you're *definitely* going to need it," he added, grinning.

◎ॐ֍

Thor remained unamused.

He stood on the deck of Gregor's yacht, his thick, ridiculously-muscular arms bulging where they folded across his chest.

He stood there, silent, scowling at her and Tyr.

Lia found it only mildly comforting that the God of Thunder didn't seem to be scowling at *her,* at least not specifically, not in a way that felt personal. Instead the entire situation seemed to anger him, at least in part because he obviously sensed some kind of trick.

In that, Lia had to admit, he definitely wasn't the only one.

"I assure you," Lia said, shaking her head at Tyr. "I'm *not* his mate. Loki stole my baby sister. He *kidnapped* her, presumably because he knew you were coming and he needed her as leverage. When I got out of the shower, he was just gone. Loki was gone, the ring was gone, and my sister was gone... and you were nearly here."

Frowning, looking around the deck, where a huge, blackened hole was now visible, now that the smoke had cleared, she rested her hands on her hips.

"I don't know he got Maia or himself off the boat."

She remembered something then, and turned, focusing on the boat's stern.

Maia had said there were three Jetskis moored there, presumably tied up on the landing area at the very back of the boat, just below the main deck of the stern.

Only one Jetski stood there now.

The other two slots were empty.

Biting her lip, Lia considered saying something, but something in her hesitated. Truthfully, she was still trying to decide if it was better to sic Thor and Tyr on Loki, or not. Maybe Loki took Maia as a warning for her not to do that exact thing.

Would Loki really hurt Maia, though?

Maybe she was delusional, but Lia hadn't gotten that impression from him at all.

Loki seemed genuinely fond of Maia.

He'd also seemed genuinely protective of her.

He'd certainly seemed genuinely angry back at the beach house when he was "teaching" Ernie not to harm underage girls.

Furious, really.

He'd been furious verging on murderous.

Hell, even now, that internal "radar" of hers—the instincts Lia depended on to survive, the same ones Loki seemed so fascinated by—even now, that radar wasn't flashing red when it came to Loki. It wasn't telling her Loki was a bad guy, or that he'd left her behind to put her in danger, or to put Maia in danger.

Then again, maybe pretending Lia's "radar" was accurate in the first place was all part of Loki's manipulation.

Still frowning, still fighting to decide, she looked back at Tyr.

"In any case, he's not my mate, I have no idea where he's gone, or why he took my sister. Not apart from what I've already told you. I assume he left me behind to slow the two of you down," she added, motioning towards the two male gods.

"...Which appears to be working."

Thor grunted, giving Tyr a dark look.

From his expression, Thor obviously agreed with Lia's assessment.

Tyr was shaking his head though, that smile ghosting his lips.

"I do not blame you for not knowing this, dear sister," Tyr said politely. "But gods cannot simply 'pretend' to mark someone as their mate. This is something they only do if they are willing to accept the lasting consequences of such an act."

Lia frowned, folding her arms.

It occurred to her that she was protecting her chest, the same part of her chest where Loki pressed his hand, not long before he disappeared.

Pushing that from her mind, she looked up at Tyr's dark eyes.

"Lasting consequences?" she grunted. "What kind of lasting consequences?"

At that, Tyr and Thor exchanged looks.

Thor still looked angry, but the amusement in Tyr's eyes, if anything, grew more prominent.

"Well," Tyr said, motioning vaguely towards her chest area. "For one thing, you *do* know where he is. He has marked you. You should be able to close your eyes, and call to him. When you do, you will see through his eyes. You will know as he knows."

Lia frowned harder, looking between the two gods.

"You're shitting me," she said.

Tyr burst out in another amused laugh, but Thor only scowled.

Still frowning, still looking between them, Lia nodded towards Thor. "Anyway, Loki told me that gods could block people from seeing them that way. He said the gods could read one another's minds... and sense them... but they could also block one another."

"He told you that?" Thor said.

Lowering his silver hammer to his side, he took a step closer to her.

Lia took a step back.

She wasn't worried about him hurting her exactly, but everything about Angry-Thor was a bit alarming.

Also, since it was only the second time he'd spoken since they'd landed, Lia jumped a little just from the god's deep, growling voice, which seemed to vibrate the air, as if charged with a wave of electric particles. Everything about that voice, including the intensity she sensed behind it, really did remind her of actual thunder and lightning.

Which, she supposed, was apt.

Still, she wasn't afraid of him *hurting* her for some reason.

Even if they were deluded enough to think she was Loki's mate.

She folded her arms tighter, jutting her chin.

"Yeah," she said. "He told me that. He told me a few things about both of you. Most of it was technical stuff. Related to running away from you both."

"When?" Thor growled. "When did he tell you these things?"

"Today," she said, blinking. "As we were leaving Gregor's house." At Thor's blank look, she added, "The one you blew up. On the cliff."

There was a silence.

Then Lia sighed, combing her fingers through her blond hair as she glanced again at the end of the boat. It hit her again, with a heaviness that time, that Loki had her kid sister.

She probably had to tell Thor and Tyr where he was.

So why was she so reluctant to do so?

Even now, she didn't want to tell them.

The thought of doing so physically pained her.

Biting her lip, she motioned vaguely towards the stern of the ship.

"He might have taken two of the Jetskis," she admitted, wincing a bit when the pain in her chest and gut sharpened.

Rubbing her belly with one hand, she scowled at Thor, then at Tyr. "I really don't know where he went. I don't want to look for him, either. Not if you're going to hurt him. Or drag him off to some jail in Asgard."

The words came out more hostile than she intended.

Really, they came out of her before she'd thought them through at all.

Biting her lip as she stared between the two males, she realized she'd spoken the truth, though. She really *didn't* want them to find Loki, with or without her help. Even though Loki had Maia. Even though Loki left her here, on her own, to deal with this crap.

Frowning as she looked between them, she fought to think.

She was still staring down at the deck of the yacht, when Tyr laid a hand on her shoulder, startling her enough that she jumped.

"It is all right, little one," he told her, his voice surprisingly warm, even affectionate. "You cannot be expected to expose your mate to danger. We both understand this." He gave Thor a pointed look. "Even if my brother is being stubborn at the moment."

"Yes," Thor growled. "And I have no reason for that whatsoever, do I, brother?"

Tyr held up a calming hand.

"I understand, brother. I do," Tyr said. "But you must admit... things are changed now. And do you not find it at least a somewhat delicious irony that they would have changed in this way? With our brother, Loki, taking a human mate? I find the whole thing rather poignant, given what he put you through with your own human mate—"

"He *left* her here," Thor growled, aiming his silver hammer at Lia. "How much could he care for her? He *left* her here! Do you think I would ever do such a thing to my dearest Sylvia?

That I would leave her with my enemies and simply 'hope for the best'?"

"His enemies?" Tyr rolled his eyes. "He left his wife with his *brothers,* Thor. Whatever our attempts to discipline him, that is hardly the same thing as 'enemy.' Do you really suppose Loki expects us to do something terrible to her?"

Pausing, Tyr looked up, focusing on the sky.

His head tilted slightly, his eyes falling out of focus as he stared up at the blue bowl overhead. After a long-feeling pause, his smile returned.

"Our brother is doing his best to block us, but he is worried. He is very, very worried about his bride here. So even knowing it is us, even knowing we would never harm her... he is far from indifferent to the situation he has left her in."

"Sure," Thor growled, setting the hammer heavily on the wooden deck. "And I'm sure he told you that, did he, brother Tyr?"

"Actually, he is not doing a very good job of blocking either of us right now, given that he very much wants to check up on his mate. You and I could likely track him easily right now, given his level of agitation."

Lia looked between the two of them, swallowing.

She folded her arms, then, feeling like the posture might be overly aggressive at this point, or maybe just overly defensive, she shoved her hands into the pockets of her shorts.

When she did, she jumped.

Staring down at her pocket, she pulled her right hand out in shock, only to shove it right back into her shorts pocket.

Fingering what she found there in a kind of amazement, she felt her throat close.

Some part of her didn't want to understand what it meant. She *did* understand, though.

Exhaling in a kind of embarrassed, frustrated, half-

outraged sigh, she pulled the ring out of her pocket and
stared at it.

She'd known without looking exactly which ring it was.

It was the same damned ring she'd stolen from Loki in
that market in Kathmandu.

It was the same ring Loki had stolen from their father,
Odin.

It was the same ring he'd stolen from his brother, Thor.

And now Lia was holding it in her hand.

PEACE OFFERING

W hen Lia glanced up, she saw Tyr staring with
amazement at the ring she held.

His dark eyes morphed into a cross between
amusement and disbelief.

Thor, who looked over a beat later, perhaps sensing something from Lia or Tyr, or just noticing the silence, stared at
her hand next.

For that first second, that's all he did.

The Thunder God stared at the ring, motionless.

Then Lia saw him blink, jumping a little in surprise, as if
he, too, was utterly shocked when it finally sank in what she
held. Walking over to her, he leaned down, staring at the
etched, bronze-and-gold-colored piece of jewelry from only a
few inches away.

He stared at it for what must have been several seconds.

Then Thor scowled.

He muttered a bunch of those strangely-melodic but
utterly foreign words under his breath, ending on something
that sounded significantly more crass and guttural.

Lia didn't have to be told the God of Thunder was likely swearing.

Even as she thought it, Thor switched to English.

"That little *shit,*" he growled, staring out over the water.

Lia glanced at Tyr, who once more looked like he was trying not to laugh.

Her eyes shifted back to Thor, who was gripping the handle of his hammer tightly again. Blue-white electric current sparked up from the hammer to his arm, coiling and twisting around his massive forearms and biceps without burning his clothes or his hair. She watched it slide around his chest, strangely fascinated, but somehow not afraid.

"You know what this means," Tyr said to Thor, his voice low.

Thor scowled, staring at his brother, staring out at sea, where he presumably expected Loki to be, at least in his mind's eye, then staring back at Lia herself, and finally the ring in her palm.

"Yes," Thor growled. "I know."

Lia held up her non-ring-bearing hand, her mouth twisting in a frown.

"Hey," she said. "I don't."

The two gods turned to her, staring down at her, and suddenly, they looked about seven feet tall, each. Swallowing, she firmed her jaw, refusing to lower her gaze.

"I mean, I know I'm supposed to give this to you," she clarified. "I'm guessing he wanted *me* to do it, thinking you'd be less likely to toss me into the ocean once I had—"

Tyr broke out in a delighted chuckle.

Lia glanced at him, but didn't stop speaking.

"—but I still feel like I'm missing something," she added. "Why didn't he just leave the ring for you here? He must have known a note would have worked as well as me."

Tyr laughed again, glancing at Thor.

The God of War patted his larger brother on the shoulder, again smiling warmly down at Lia.

"I believe you are far more of a message than the Andvaranaut, my clever, beautiful new sister," Tyr said, grinning. At her confused look, he clarified, "The ring. What you are holding in your hand. Yes, we are here to retrieve it, and yes, I think you are right that he means for you to give it to us. But I think the message he would like to send is that he has a human mate now. It is a peace offering, but also a request of his brothers. And ultimately a request of our father."

"A request?" Lia frowned, glancing at Thor, still holding the ring flat on her palm. "You mean, 'here's your ring back... don't beat the crap out of me?'" she said. "That kind of request?"

Tyr let out another delighted chuckle.

Thor gave her a hard look with those ice-blue eyes, but Lia couldn't help noticing that something in them had softened, and perhaps not only to her.

"It's a bit more nuanced than that, sister," the blond god with the massive shoulders said. Raking his fingers through his long hair, he let out a defeated-sounding sigh. "...but that's the gist of it, yes. Loki is attempting to parlay with us. And doing his usual... apologizing without *actually* apologizing. Especially to me."

"Apologizing?" She blinked down at the ring. "You mean for stealing this?"

Tyr snorted another laugh.

"More for what he did to Thor's *own* human wife," the God of War explained. "And his scoffing dismissal of our brother being mated to a human in the first place—"

"Which is what?" Lia frowned, feeling slightly alarmed, and slightly worried, in spite of herself. "What did Loki do to Thor's wife?"

Thor turned, glaring at Tyr, then a little less menacingly at her.

"Oh," Thor said sarcastically. "Not much. Your husband only gave my wife to his sociopathic, shape-shifting, water dragon son. Told Jörmungandr to *breed* with her to create a demigod ruler of Earth. No biggie. I mean, he let his son kidnap her and take her to Alfheim, locking her inside an underwater prison... but, you know, he *really wanted that ring* you've got on your hand right now..."

Thor aimed the hammer at where she still held out her palm.

"...so I guess it's all understandable, right?"

Lia swallowed, staring up at those angry, pale-blue eyes.

"Oh," she said meekly.

"Yes. 'Oh.'"

Thor glared at Tyr when the other god chuckled again.

Thor continued to stare at his brother a few seconds longer, mouth hard, as if daring him to say another word. Then the God of Thunder turned his wrath back on Lia. Strangely, however, that anger still didn't feel aimed at her.

It more felt like Thor *really* wanted to be yelling at Loki.

He aimed those words at Lia instead—likely in a much-restrained voice, compared to how he'd be saying these things if Loki stood in front of him—probably because she was the only one there. She found herself thinking Thor might hope she'd convey the message back to Loki as well, or even that Loki might somehow feel Thor's message through her.

"Now my brother," Thor added sourly. "My charming, utterly infuriating brother, who put my wife in such danger, would clearly like to convey to me he's seen the error of his ways. He wants me to know he's found *himself* a human wife he wants, and that he'll give the ring back, abandon his plans to subjugate the human race... all for the low, low price of being let off scot-free to live his life happily with the woman

he loves, with no prison time in Asgard, no banishment to the outer worlds, and no banishment from Earth..."

Grunting at Tyr's laugh, Thor scowled back at Lia.

"According to Loki, this should settle things. He expects me to sympathize with him because of you, accept his apology, and lobby our father on his behalf that we should all just let bygones be bygones."

Thor growled his opinion of this, even as Tyr snorted another laugh.

When Lia glanced at Tyr, however, quirking an eyebrow, the dark-eyed god nodded sympathetically, as if he agreed with Thor's assessment.

"Our brother has a... unique... way of communicating," Tyr explained. "I suspect his message to us is more or less exactly what my brother, Thor, just said. Loki clearly adores you, chose you as his mate, and now wishes us to fuck off back to our own lives and sections of the cosmos, and leave him and his new bride alone."

Grinning a little, Tyr shrugged at Thor's glare, holding up his hands.

"You have to admit, brother. It's a *little* funny."

"It is outrageous!" Thor growled.

"You say that as if Loki isn't *always* outrageous," Tyr pointed out. "You cannot ask him to be what he is not. But look at the imprint he has left on his new mate. Clearly, he is utterly smitten. Would you really deprive him of that?"

Tyr's voice lowered, growing more serious.

"Because honestly, brother? I think you would not. I think none of us would. When is the last time Loki had love in his life? *Real* love? Are you really going to pretend that such a thing would not exert a positive influence on him?"

Thor glared at Tyr.

He opened his mouth to answer, but Tyr held up a hand.

"I said *love,* brother," Tyr said, his voice warning. "Not

lust. Not whatever the hell he did to create Jörmungandr or
Fenrir. Or what he did to trick our father in Alfheim that one
time. I mean the love it would take to mark this one as his
mate."

Thor closed his mouth, scowling.

He looked at Lia, aiming that scowl at her.

At the same time, she saw that softer look in Thor's eyes,
too, as he examined whatever it was they saw of their brother
on Lia. His reaction to that thing, whatever it was, seemed to
irritate the blond god even more.

It also seemed to leave him resigned.

Like Tyr said, Thor didn't seem capable of ignoring it.

Finally, he scowled at Lia.

"Fine," he said. "Give me the ring, if you please."

He held out a thick hand, his blue eyes blazing.

Lia tilted her own hand over it, letting the gold and
bronze circlet fall into the meatiest part of the god's palm.
Thor's fingers closed over the ring, right before he disappeared it somewhere on his person, Lia guessed in the pocket
of his black suit pants.

"Thank you," Thor said, gruff. "And apologies, sister.
Congratulations. I hope it is clear it is not you I take issue
with, but your incorrigible mate."

Lia smiled, maybe for the first time since she found Loki
gone.

"Oh, I'd like to have a few words with him myself, right
now," she muttered, glancing out over the water and waves
towards the shores of California.

When she glanced back at the two gods, both of them
burst out in a laugh.

Even Thor laughed that time, throwing back his head.

As he did, however, he made a more frustrated sound, like
he still wasn't sure if he wanted to strangle something,
continue laughing about it, or just let the whole thing go.

Thor and Tyr looked at each other then, and something seemed to pass between them. At the end of it, Tyr shrugged, holding up his hands, and Thor scowled, but that hotter look in his eyes finally seemed to be fading for real.

"Fine," he growled, turning to Lia. "Tell Loki I will bring the ring back to Asgard, and speak to our father on his behalf. Tell him, I make no promises as to what Odin will say. Much less what he will do. Or if he will accept this half-assed apology in any way."

Lia felt herself paling, losing some of the blood from her face.

Tyr must have noticed, because he immediately spoke up.

"Thor can make no promises, it is true," the God of War said, his voice shifting to a more reassuring tone. "However, our father, as a general rule, does not interfere once the issue of mates becomes involved. It is one of those unspoken things, but I have never known him to act differently. Loki is no doubt counting on his father to offer him some clemency in this case, because of you."

"And because he's the bloody favorite," Thor growled. "Even after all this time."

Tyr rolled his eyes, giving Thor a sideways look.

"Our father is fond of all of us." Tyr glanced at Thor, quirking an eyebrow. "For example, he recently released Thor from his normal duties on Asgard and in the other realms, all so he can spend time with his mate here on Earth. I suspect Odin will overlook Loki's transgressions for similar reasons."

Lia blinked. "Because of me? Why would I have anything to do with it?"

Rather than Tyr, Thor answered her, his voice booming.

For the first time, a faint note of humor lived in his words.

"If nothing else, our father knows he finally has *leverage* over the miscreant," Thor said, giving her a wan smile. "I suspect that alone will still Odin's hand. Loki knows if he ever got out of line, Odin could separate the two of you... which, once a god has bonded with a mate, is a kind of torture for us. Truthfully, as much as I hate to admit it, it says something indeed that Loki would make us aware of you. It is a form of offering the jugular—especially to someone like Loki, who hates appearing vulnerable in any way. My brother Tyr is likely right, for this reason alone. Loki would only do this if he intended to keep his word."

Lia nodded, her brow clearing.

Thinking, she added, "But you'd still like to *thunk* him on the head with that thing." Lia pointed at the silver hammer. "...Right?"

That time, Thor let out a real laugh.

Lia stepped back in reflex, a little alarmed at the deep, near-roar that came out of the blue-eyed god's chest. Thor only smiled at her when he lowered his head, and she found herself a little thrown, seeing how much that smile transformed his face.

"Yes, little sister," the God of Thunder said, smiling wider. He winked at her, hefting his hammer up on one bulging shoulder. "I would very much like to *thunk* him on the head. Several times, in fact. Right before I threw him off this boat."

Tyr chuckled, smacking Thor on the shoulder playfully before he aimed his smile at Lia.

As he did, Lia felt another presence there, a worried-feeling presence, somewhere in the back of her mind. The presence pooled in her chest as liquid warmth, and Lia could almost see Loki there, his light green eyes looking through her darker green ones at his two brothers.

She felt Loki assess the situation.

She felt the exact instant he made up his mind about what he was seeing.

Relief flooded through her then, filling her chest, her throat, warming her face and belly. That relief remained tinged with a sharper, denser bite of worry, but the edges of that smoothed the longer he watched his brothers smile at her.

She found herself wondering if Loki knew she could feel him there.

She found herself wondering if she was losing her mind, imagining things.

Perhaps not for that. The Trickster God smiled at her, winking inside her mind. *But certainly for allowing me to make you my mate, little elf.*

Is that what I did? Lia thought dryly. *Allow you to make me your mate?*

Most certainly. It is an entirely mutual event. By definition.

Sighing a bit, and deciding to let it go for the moment, Lia combed her fingers through her long blond hair, looking out towards the ocean.

So we're okay, then? Lia thought at him next, still aiming her smile at Thor and Tyr. *They're not going to whisk you away to an Asgardian prison if you come back here? Or if I look away for a few minutes? Or in a week? Or after a few months have gone by?*

No, no. My brothers are hardly perfect, but they are not liars.

Then bring my damned sister back, Loki, she thought at him, sharper, making her thoughts deliberately louder as she gritted her teeth. *Now. Or I might throw you into the ocean myself. Naked. Covered in fish guts to attract the sharks.*

Pausing at his delighted laugh, even as that warm presence in her chest grew hotter, more dense, more filled with desire and affection, Lia added,

And if you ever leave me like that again, without telling me a damned thing, you'd better sleep with one eye open, God of Mischief.

Hey, Loki thought back at her. *You knew who you married.*

Without knowing I was MARRIED AT ALL, she retorted.

Feeling Loki's amusement grow in equal amounts with that hotter, denser reaction, Lia sighed. It was impossible to stay angry though, as much as she might have wanted. That liquid heat continued to fill her chest, what felt like desire mixed with affection mixed with... well, other things, perhaps emotions stronger than lust *or* affection...

Pushing it briefly out of her mind, Lia refocused on Tyr.

The God of War was smiling at her again.

Lia saw the knowingness in that smile, the amusement that lived there.

More than that, the understanding.

Realizing Loki's brother must have picked up on her talking to Loki, she blushed.

Chuckling a little, Tyr only smiled wider, wrapping his arm around her shoulders, squeezing her to his side in a hug.

"It is all right, sister," Tyr whispered in her ear. "I don't blame my brother for keeping a close eye on you."

Immediately, Lia felt an annoyed burst of heat off Loki.

Tell flirty brother McFlirty to kindly keep his hands to himself, the god muttered. *Tell him he's about to get a black eye... or perhaps a broken knee... or perhaps some Alfheim sand fleas in his sock and underwear drawer for the next several centuries...*

Lia stifled a smile, rolling her eyes.

You're an idiot, she informed the god.

And you are a wholly disobedient, problematic human, he told her. *Tell him what I said. Tell him now. And stop touching him. He's a shameless flirt... but I wouldn't put it past him to act on it, if only to annoy me.*

Lia snorted, shaking her head.

Leaning into Tyr's side, she folded her arms, gazing out at the California shore, watching the waves roll under and around the yacht.

Despite what Loki said, she felt absolutely nothing weird from Tyr. Furthermore, she wasn't about to brush off his brother, just because Loki was a paranoid freak.

Lia— the god growled.

Let's just nip that in the bud right here, Trickster God, she thought at him. *If you expect total obedience from me, or for me to avoid all other men for the rest of eternity, or even for me to dutifully play my assigned role in little dramas like this one on a regular basis, we need to have a talk about this whole "mate" business.*

It's too late for that.

Is it? Lia snorted. *Is it, really? Because your brothers are still here. As in RIGHT HERE. As in, I could tell them I have absolutely no intention of being your mate, and intend to ask you to undo whatever weirdness you did to me to convince them to believe it.*

There was a silence in her mind.

In that silence, Lia felt Loki back down.

She felt him acknowledge her words, even as his presence somehow shifted, growing more submissive, more conscious of the two male gods with her.

It also turned a lot more grumbly.

Feeling that, Lia fought another laugh.

Jeez, Loks, she thought at him, rolling her eyes. *Are Asgardian jails really that bad? Is it really worth shoving yourself into a marriage you didn't intend, just to avoid one?*

There was another silence.

You think that's why I did this? he thought back.

He actually sounded offended.

Lia felt her amused smile fade as he went on.

I give up my plans to design a perfect Earth, he thought at her. *Hand my brothers and my control-freak father the ultimate leverage over me. Eat crow by admitting I let myself fall in love. And your response is to accuse me of orchestrating the whole thing just to avoid being caught? By two brothers who had absolutely NO IDEA where I was until you crossed my path? Really? That's your ultimate conclusion, Lia Winchester?*

Biting her lip to keep from smiling, she watched him glare at her from his mind.

She could almost see those leaf-green eyes.

For your information, my darling, my love, light of my world, I NEVER WOULD HAVE BEEN CAUGHT. I could have eluded them forever down here. Easily. I could do it now, and steal the ring AGAIN, if I was willing to leave you behind. I could have done precisely what I told you I would do with that ring, without Thor or Tyr ever catching up to me, or knowing how I'd inserted myself in the human world. So you've got it all completely backwards, love. Really, you should be terribly flattered—

Should I? she thought back, amused. *Flattered? Really?*

Terribly, he reiterated. *It is all utterly unprecedented. A ridiculous compliment. Furthermore, I thought you knew me better. I thought you knew I could EASILY outsmart my two brothers... my modesty about Tyr's intellect as compared to my own notwithstanding.*

Lia snorted again, shaking her head at a man who wasn't there.

At the same time, some deeper, stranger, perhaps slightly masochistic part of herself almost believed him, and *almost* was a tiny bit affected by his words.

Maybe even a little bit touched.

She still understood why Thor wanted to *thunk* him on the head, though.

She suspected she might want to do that herself, from time to time.

FATHER OF MISCHIEF

"**N**ow in German..." the patient voice said, languid in the late afternoon sun.

Lia heard a mumbled response from a younger, significantly more female voice.

She didn't make out the exact words of that response, since she was still walking across the hand-painted tiles that covered their indoor patio, heading for the open, double French doors that led to outside. Pushing through those same doors, Lia joined the two of them on the enormous stone balcony in their Parisian apartment overlooking the Seine.

Seeing her little sister, Maia, sitting there primly, books in her lap, blue eyes serious as she gazed at the man across from her, Lia smiled, in spite of herself.

Then she looked at the man instructing Maia, and rolled her eyes, snorting.

Loki had an arm folded behind his head, cushioning his skull where he stretched out on a yellow and pale blue striped sun lounger. She noticed he'd moved the lounger since she'd last been up here, re-positioning the outdoor furniture such that it got a full dose of direct sunlight from the yellow orb in the sky.

He wore designer sunglasses. A black, collared shirt open at the neck displayed his distinctive band of black and gold, runic tattoos. Burgundy pants clung to his long legs. Italian shoes adorned his feet.

Adjusting his head on his arm, he seemed to look only at Maia.

"German, pet," Loki repeated, his voice a touch warning. "That was Russian. As you *very well* know. Let's try it in German, first—"

"Just how many languages are you teaching her?" Lia mused.

She plopped down on the lounger next to him, handing him a mocha cappuccino. She'd made it exactly the way he liked it, with four shots of expresso, whole milk, fresh whipped cream and chocolate shavings on top.

"I thought it was just French and Spanish this week," she added, watching him take a sip of the coffee, grin at her, then lean up to deliver a kiss on her mouth.

"I could ravage you right here," he said, reaching for her. "Marry me. For this coffee alone. Marry me, and I will slaver you in exotic cheeses..."

Maia laughed.

Lia pushed his hand away, grinning.

"...Two languages aren't enough?" she continued, undaunted, drawing away from a second kiss. "Don't you think she should get French down first, considering where we're living?"

Loki sighed, leaning back on the striped lounger.

"Tut-tut, my love," he said, setting the coffee mug on a small glass table. "...and no, no, no, no. I assume you are joking. That will *never* do. Our little piglet must simply

SHINE and surpass, no matter what school she attends, no matter what country we reside in. She must blind and deafen EVERY OTHER human cub with her superior intellect and skills. She must show the bland nothings of your species, particularly those with whom she shares a classroom, that she is their intellectual, moral, and cultural superior in every way—"

Lia burst out in a laugh.

"So this is your new plan for world domination? Turning my sister into some kind of sleeper agent to take over humanity?"

"Whyever not? She's *obviously* the most superior specimen of your species already. Well... apart from you, and I'm too greedy to use you for such things." He tugged at Lia's blond hair, smiling at Maia. "She's splendid. Already head and shoulders above all the other rug-rats. She only needs a little coaching is all..."

That time, Maia huffed at him.

"I'm getting straight A's," the younger Winchester informed him, indignant.

She sat up straighter where she perched on the lounger on Loki's other side, still wearing her school uniform. Lia assumed she must have come straight up here after walking home from the nearby academy.

Presumably to find Loki—not her, as in Lia herself.

"I'm the third best in my class," Maia said proudly.

"Ah, you see?" Loki lowered his sunglasses, looking first at Maia, then back at Lia. "She is falling horribly, terribly, *embarrassingly* behind, and it's only been a month. I blame myself entirely. This is simply NOT acceptable. We can't have two, whole, ordinary humans boasting of their superiority! No! I will not permit it! I will not stand for it!"

Seeing the faint smile at his lips, Lia burst out in a laugh, sliding onto his sun lounger to share it with him. When he scooted over to accommodate her, Lia leaned her head on his shoulder, sighing a bit in spite of herself.

"You're a nut," she told him, feeling her muscles relax. "And stop teasing poor Maia! She's going to think you're serious."

"No, I won't," Maia insisted.

Scooting over a few more inches to make room for her, Loki wrapped an arm around Lia's back, squeezing her against him and caressing the strip of bare skin between her fitted, lime-green, recently-bought pants and the bottom of her cropped halter top.

Both articles of clothing, along with her slip-on flats, were ridiculously expensive.

She found them in a designer boutique while on one of her wanders with Loki, and he'd insisted on getting them for her when she mentioned in passing she thought they were cute.

She still hadn't gotten used to the money.

Never, not once in Lia's life until now, had money *not* been an issue.

She'd been a professional thief, but the vast majority of her spoils always went to someone else, to provide luxuries for someone else. Before now, it seemed like all she *did* was worry about money. Mostly, she worried about how she would ever get enough together to buy Maia's freedom.

She was still getting used to not having to worry about that.

She was still getting used to not having to worry about a lot of things.

"You're one of those parents," Lia teased, glancing up at Loki without giving up her comfy position with her head on his shoulder. "Joke all you want, but you really are. I never in a million years would have guessed you'd be one of *those* parents."

"Which parents, my love?"

"A hyper-driven, super-involved, psychotically-motivated *super-crazy* parent who thinks their kid can do anything."

"Maia *can* do anything," Loki said, indignant.

"Yeah," Maia said, sticking her tongue out at Lia.

"Besides," Loki said. "I insist all of my children excel at everything they attempt."

Maia looked faintly outraged at that, turning her stare on Loki.

"I'm not a *child.*"

"You are most *certainly* a child," Loki countered, looking over his sunglasses at her. "You are your sister's ward, which makes you a sort of pseudo-offspring of hers, if I'm understanding the legal technicalities of child management on this world. That is the legal *truth* of the thing, even if you are biologically siblings."

Pausing, Loki added, with a flourish of his hand,

"Being your sister's mate, and her official snuggle-bunny, that makes you MY ward, little Maia... a *stepfather,* if you will. And I insist ALL OF MY OFFSPRING be equipped to face any and all unexpected contingencies in life. Regardless of their age or exact species."

"Species?" Maia giggled.

"Precisely. Do you know you have a brother who is a shape-shifting water dragon? And another who is a giant wolf?"

"You're crazy," Maia told him.

Loki winked at her, wrapping his arm tighter about Lia.

"I love only your mother, however," he said. "So you are, of course, my favorite. Do not tell my other children that, however, or one of them might eat you. They are quite possessive."

Lia smacked Loki on the chest, but Maia seemed to have lost interest in her demi-god and full-god step-siblings. She was focused back on her own preoccupations with Loki.

"So teach me more about picking locks," Maia complained. "You said you would."

"Wait, what?" Lia lifted her head, staring between her and Loki. "Maia, no! Absolutely not! Loki isn't teaching you that!"

"Why not?" her younger sister said, motioning at Loki. "He *promised* he would. He said he'd teach me once I made some progress on French. He *also* promised to teach me how to shoot the guns you guys have hidden in the locked closet. And how to fight people with knives. And how to break passwords. And how to hack computers..."

Lia's eyebrows rose higher and higher.

She looked at Loki, who smiled at her faintly from behind the sunglasses, shrugging as he squeezed her tighter against him.

"The little peanut must be prepared for life," he said, matter-of-fact. "It is a brutal, uncaring world you've brought her into, my pet. She won't always have Stepfather Loki there to pull disgusting perverted humans off her. She won't always have Stepfather Loki there to rescue her from beachside mansions, after she is kidnapped to act as leverage against her sister who is being blackmailed to pay off a multi-million dollar debt left by her backstabbing mother who cheated a cruel mobster..."

Lia rolled her eyes, but Maia burst out in another spate of giggles.

Loki looked at Maia over his sunglasses, smiling fondly.

When he glanced at Lia, she pursed her lips, quirking her eyebrow at him.

"So you're turning my kid sister into an assassin?" Lia said. "That doesn't strike you as slightly... extreme?"

"I expect ALL of my children to be able to pull their own

weight," Loki repeated loftily. "Anyway, you'll give her an inferiority complex, otherwise... my darling, talented, slightly terrifying wife. I can't have my little pincushion feeling like she wasn't given the same advantages in life as big sis."

"Advantages?" Lia smacked his arm, half-amused, half-outraged. "Is that what you call it? *Advantages?* Really?"

"How many languages do you speak, dearest?" Loki asked her, now staring at her over the expensive, orange-tinted shades.

Lia frowned, thinking. "Five?"

"And can you fire various guns and rifles and such?"

"Well... yeah."

"You are a talented thief. An excellent getaway driver. A safe-cracker who is quite good with explosives, knives—"

"I *had* to learn all of that stuff," Lia reminded him, poking him in the chest. "I had absolutely no choice. And nothing remotely like a normal childhood."

"PRECISELY," Loki said, laughing as he pushed her poking finger away. "Which is why I must overcompensate in teaching our dear little platypus here. Why would you not wish me to teach the same skills that proved so valuable to you, to our adorable, clever, tricky little ward? She's a positive sponge with your brains and her own unfettered innocence... is she not? Why not load her up with as many life skills as we can? She'll likely hate both of us in a few years anyway, and run off with a biker named Thad. Or worse... a televangelist."

Loki shuddered.

Maia burst out in another laugh, and the god winked at her, grinning his shark's grin under the orange-tinted glasses.

Lia sighed, leaning her chin on the hand she rested on Loki's chest.

When she glanced at her sister, Maia was grinning triumphantly at her.

The younger Winchester clearly sensed her impending win.

"You *are* kind of my mom now," Maia reminded her innocently. "Which makes *him* kind of my dad. And makes it *your job* to prepare me for the world. You can't exactly get mad at him, just because he's being *practical*—"

"Oh, for crying out loud," Lia complained, looking between them, her chin still resting on Loki's chest. "You're ganging up on me. You're *already* ganging up on me... and tag-teaming to push through your shady agendas. And you're both far, FAR too pleased about it."

"Only because we know what a softie you are," Loki smiled, stroking her cheek with the backs of his fingers.

Leaning down, he kissed her tenderly on the mouth.

"A softie?" Lia grunted, tugging on his long red and black hair, watching him smile at her as he stared at her through the sunglasses. "I don't think letting you turn my baby sister into some kind of ninja-spy-assassin-thief exactly qualifies me for being labeled a 'softie.'"

"How about my dear, sweet wife, who I would do absolutely anything for?" Loki said.

"Everything except stop teaching my baby sister how to do things that could land her in jail," Lia grumbled, resting her chin back on his chest. "...Apparently."

Loki grinned at her, caressing the small of her back, kneading the muscle there with his fingers and watching her face as she relaxed into him.

After a few more seconds of that, she felt a different part of him pressing into her belly, even as he stretched slightly under her, pressing into her more. She wrapped her arms around him, telling herself it was to cover him up so Maia didn't see anything, even as she shifted closer on the lounger, feeling his muscles tense as he reacted.

Loki turned his head lazily towards Maia, his voice casual.

"Run along now, little turnip," he said, his voice equally lazy. "Mommy and Daddy need to talk privately now."

Maia raised an eyebrow, looking between them.

"Talk privately?" She snorted. "Is that some kind of code? What? Are you going to argue more about my ninja training?"

"No, no." Loki shooed her away with a hand. "Mommy and Daddy stuff. Go down and do your homework. Don't come up until it's all finished. Then I'll see if I can work on big sis to take you out to the gun range."

Maia's eyes lit up and Lia smacked him on the chest.

"You are impossible," she told him, speaking into his ear.

When Maia gathered up her school books and backpack, dragging them back towards the French doors, Lia smacked Loki on the chest again, even as he grinned at her through the designer sunglasses, his long hair hanging nearly to his shoulders, but shorter than when she'd first met him.

He looked almost "European" now, versus full-blown barbarian.

Loki pushed her aside and stood up from the lounger before she could really lay into him. She watched him walk to the French doors and close them, pulling across a set of curtains they'd had installed on the outside.

Lia watched, eyebrows raised, as he dragged one of the palm tree pots in front of the outward-opening doors, making it so Maia couldn't surprise them.

"We could go inside, you know," Lia remarked, watching him with some amusement. "Rather than giving the neighbors a show."

"Oh, I can glamour us for that. Don't want to traumatize the little tot, though, if she comes up here and finds us missing…"

Shaking her head bemusedly, Lia watched him walk back to her.

She couldn't help noticing, not for the first time, he had

the strange, catlike, verging-on-feral step that she'd noticed on his brother, Tyr.

If anything, Loki moved even more like that.

It was as if he moved through the edges of life, only visible when he wanted to be.

"Are you missing your cat-burglar ways, my love?" he asked her, watching her look at him. "Are you tempted to pick my pocket right now?"

"I'm wondering how long before you get bored, my little love-bunny," she told him wryly, realizing as she said it that the worry was real.

It nagged at some part of her, tugging at the back of her mind.

It had, more or less, since she'd met him.

"You don't seem like one for the domestic life..." she added apologetically.

Loki looked faintly appalled. He threw himself down on the sun lounger next to her, without taking his eyes off her face.

"Are you disappointed in my parenting skills, love?" he said. "For real? I thought this tug of war of ours was all in good fun."

"No." Lia shook her head, sighing. "That's not it. Not at all."

She met his gaze when he lifted his sunglasses to his forehead, watching her worriedly.

"Maia adores you," Lia added. "She positively *adores* you. I think that's what worries me. If you couldn't do this anymore, she would be devastated."

"*She* would be devastated?" He frowned, looking even more worried.

"*I* would be devastated," Lia corrected. "*We* would be devastated."

Loki blinked, staring at her.

"Is this a regular worry of yours?" he said. "My leaving you?"

Lia tilted her head, sliding back onto his chest, caressing the parts of it exposed by the open shirt. "It's crossed my mind," she admitted.

Wrapping his arm around her, he tugged her higher up his body, sliding a hand around her face, and into her hair. He kissed her mouth, pulling on her with his tongue and lips, coaxing her into him as he deepened the kiss.

By the end of it, by the time he pulled away, Lia's skin felt hot all over. She was out of breath, her eyes half-lidded as she looked at him.

"That's not helping," she told him, smiling.

"Isn't it?"

"Giving me more things to miss if you left?" she said. "No."

He smiled at her wanly.

Then his eyes, mouth and voice abruptly grew stern, uncompromising. He gripped her hair in his fingers, staring up at her eyes.

"I love you, little elf," he told her, shaking her hair and head lightly in his fingers. "I love you very, very much. Do you love me?"

Lia swallowed, looking into those leaf-green eyes.

"You've never said that to me before," she said. "I mean, jokingly, sure, to Maia—"

"You think I am *joking* when I tell Maia I love you? Or when I tell her that I love her?"

Lia frowned. "You tell Maia that?"

"Of course I tell Maia that! What kind of terrible parent do you think I am?"

Lia blinked at him. "It's just... you never really said it to me. Not like this, I mean. Not when we're alone, and you're being remotely serious."

"Which, clearly, was an egregious error... one that's caused you to entirely misunderstand my purpose in being here, on this world. Apparently you humans need everything spelled out in neon lights. I may have a parade for you, Lia Winchester... right down the Avenue des Champs-Élysées, with elephants, and jugglers, and dancing bears. A mariachi band and several French crooners singing my undying love. At least one rap band detailing how I would love to defile you for the rest of my days..."

When Lia burst out in a laugh, smacking his chest, he smiled.

"Did you really not understand the deal I made with my brothers? Or why?" he said, watching her eyes. "Come now, dearest. I thought it was clear to you, just how momentous that decision was for me."

Lia sighed a bit.

"Your decision not to take over the world, you mean?" she said.

"Precisely."

When she snorted a laugh, Loki shook her again lightly, bringing her eyes back to his.

"Lover," he said, soft, kissing her mouth. "You laugh, but I really did feel my father had made a tremendous mistake with your world and your species."

Pausing as he studied her eyes, he added,

"YOU, Lia Winchester, made me actually *believe* in my father's experiment. For the first time, I saw the *benefits* of this free will of yours, despite the chaos and war, the horrid things done to your oceans and rivers, the disgusting smoke in most of your air. Despite the rank stupidity of many in your race. Despite the destruction they cause when they operate unchecked. Despite the dangers to our little rabbit downstairs because of it..."

Lia smiled, brushing the hair off his neck, massaging the top of his chest.

"You really are okay, being with us for a while?" she said, soft.

"I love you," he repeated.

Looking around them in exasperation, he threw up his hands.

"I'm definitely having the parade. Maybe a forty-gun salute. With pirate ships. And fireworks at the end of the night... with cannons firing their weapons into the sea."

Laughing, Lia smacked him, but he caught ahold of her face, pulling her closer.

They kissed for longer that time, and Lia found herself flushing for real, her hands exploring Loki where he lay under her, until he was groaning against her mouth, pressing against her urgently as he began to undress her.

He had the halter-top off, the bra on the cement balcony floor, not far from the white stone pillars with vines wrapped around them. He unfastened her pants next, and she sat up to help him get them off, even as she tugged his shirt off his muscular shoulders, making him gasp when he pulled her up against him.

Her heart was beating so hard now, she could almost hear it.

When she glanced up, he was looking at her, his green eyes serious, stripped of any of that wry humor she usually saw there, or the more mischievous look he often wore.

His fingers rose to her face.

He used the back of them to trace her cheek and jaw, caressing her softly.

That more serious look burned hotter as he looked at her.

"I adore you," he told her, studying her eyes. "I absolutely adore you, little elf... and I would be devastated if we were ever separated. I'm already hatching schemes whereby I might extend your life to that of a god's. Or perhaps find some way to have you reincarnate into Asgard, as my brother wishes with his human wife."

Lia swallowed, studying his face.

She saw no lie there.

Nothing in that radar of hers told her he was lying, or that anything was wrong.

As she watched him look at her, a smile broke out over her face.

That part of her that normally sat coiled, waiting for some kind of disaster to strike, for some person she loved to leave her—like her father had, then her mother, then everyone else she'd let herself trust—wound around Loki like a cat, purring contently.

"I belong to you, little elf," he told her, kissing her tenderly on the mouth. "I belong to you as long as you'll have me. Perhaps longer than you would wish."

Kissing her again, he withdrew his head so he could look at her.

His eyes remained faintly worried, she noticed.

As if he read her thoughts, the God of Mischief added,

"Now stop worrying me! Stop making me paranoid I'm a bad mate, and a worse husband and father, or I'll throw a parade for you every day for the next ten years, trying to prove it to you... which will cut into our sex time horribly, and likely Maia's education fund, despite my ample money-making talents..."

Lia burst out in a laugh, wrapping her arms around his neck, and Loki kissed her again.

That time, he didn't stop for quite a long time.

WANT MORE LOKI AND LIA?
Grab the FREE bonus epilogue!

Just click the link to get your FREE bonus story with Loki
and Lia:

https://bit.ly/Loki-Epilogue

WANT TO READ MORE NORSE GODS?
Check out the next book in the GODS ON EARTH series!

TYR
Gods on Earth #3

Link: https://bit.ly/GOE03-eb

I'm trying to save her life.
I'm trying to stop a war.
But nothing about Marion Ravenscroft is easy.
And the world wants to careen into war, no matter what
I do.

I'm out of practice in dealing with human women.

Especially human women who do strip teases for me, the first time I meet them. Especially human women I feel strangely drawn to, pulled into, like I knew her before I even met her. Especially human women who won't do a damned thing I say.

I'm Tyr, God of War, son of Odin.

I'm supposed to be the adult in the room. Among my brothers, I'm the one who is duty-bound to keep the humans from destroying themselves, to keep peace among their tribes. Yet it was Loki who sent me on this quest, when his new wife stumbled upon a plot to kidnap the daughter of the President of the United States.

It should have been an easy way to stop a war. A simple tracking job. A simple rescue. I deliver Marion to her father, and then I deal with the dark forces attempting to harm her.

But Marion won't let me save her.

She also might be the thing to finally make me lose my cool.

See below for sample pages!

FREE DOWNLOAD!

Grab a copy of KIREV'S DOOR, the exciting backstory of the main character from my "Quentin Black" series, when he's still a young slave on "his" version of Earth. Plus seven other stories, many of which you can't get anywhere else!!

⭐⭐⭐⭐⭐

This box set is TOTALLY EXCLUSIVE to those who sign up for my VIP mailing list, "The Light Brigade!"

GET MY FREE BOOK!

Or go to: https://www.jcandrijeski.com/mailing-list

REVIEWS ARE AUTHOR HUGS

Now that you've finished reading my book,
PLEASE CONSIDER LEAVING A REVIEW!
A short review is fine and so very appreciated.
Word of mouth is truly essential for any author to succeed!

Leave a Review Here:
https://bit.ly/GOE02-eb

SAMPLE PAGES
TYR (Gods on Earth #3)

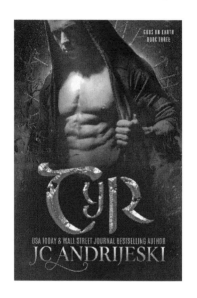

1 / THE MEETING

TYR SAT AT A HUMAN BAR, in a human drinking establishment, in a human city.

Which meant, naturally, he was on the human world.

The brother he hadn't expected to see, at least not anytime soon, and certainly not in any kind of *work* capacity, called to him the day before.

He proposed he and Tyr meet.

Tyr looked around at the location Loki had given him, and frowned.

The location wasn't the problem.

A hole in the wall pub, in Paris' University District, the bar itself presented as comfortable and private enough. It wasn't Loki's usual sort of place—the God of Mischief tended to gravitate towards flashier, more expensive, and frankly *gaudier* places, in Tyr's experience. Loki also generally preferred sitting outside, in the sun, or at least under excellent lighting. Thor used to mutter that the God of Mischief could easily have been named God of the Sun, if he wasn't such an annoying and unapologetically irredeemable wanker.

Of course, Thor muttered such things less, these days.

Tyr himself had no quarrel with a neighborhood bar, filled with guests who generally kept to themselves, who generally weren't there to be seen.

No, it was Loki himself who caused Tyr to frown.

His brother, his normally cheerful, happy-go-lucky, give-no-shits brother—maddeningly so, from some in the family's perspective—had sounded uncharacteristically serious, even somber, when Tyr finally reached him over the telephone.

Tyr wasn't sure he wanted to know what brought that urgency to Loki's voice, or the worry he'd felt in his brother's heart in the short time they spoke.

Whatever was on Loki's mind, it concerned him enough that he'd felt the need to meet with Tyr in person. Granted, Loki asked Tyr to come to Paris—where Loki currently lived—versus offering to go to Tyr himself, but still, even with that Loki-like detail, it was strange.

Loki *had* changed though, in the last few months.

The God of Mischief had a new life, with a brand-new human wife, and even a sort of daughter, in the form of his new wife's young sister and ward.

Tyr wondered if Loki's new family might be the *real* reason for his brother's worry.

Clearly, the stakes had changed for the God of Mischief when it came to Earth. The stakes had changed even more dramatically regarding the fate of the human race.

The fact that Loki called Tyr suggested a few things.

Being the God of War, most assumed Tyr's job was to *foster* conflict.

Tyr's primary job, in fact, was to avoid it.

It seemed a never-ending task, like rolling a boulder up a steep mountain, as Sisyphus did in that myth of the Greeks... or doing the dishes, or laundry, or simply keeping oneself fed on a world such as this one, where food was required.

Loki knew Tyr's true role, however.

If Loki was bringing something to Tyr, it likely meant Loki found something he felt could be problematic for the human race.

Perhaps even catastrophic.

Tyr checked his human watch, which was expensive, silver, and went with the tailored human suit he wore to blend in on Earth.

Loki was late.

Tyr was about to call out to his brother, to see if he was within psychic earshot, so to speak, when the door to the drinking establishment opened with a bang, and a tall man with black and auburn hair walked in, wearing a long coat, dark green pants and a matching jacket, a black dress shirt, a black tie, Italian boots, a gold watch and cufflinks.

His haircut alone looked like it cost an indecent amount, possibly even several hundred Euros.

As per usual, Loki managed to both blend in and dramatically stick out.

He had the human schtick down perfectly, perhaps a little too well. Loki also drew eyes, as a matter of course, for all kinds of reasons. Some element of Loki's make-up drank that attention in, which only encouraged it more.

His pale green eyes scanned the inside of the human establishment, then lit upon Tyr.

A smile curved that full mouth, one that didn't reach his leaf-green eyes.

He walked briskly in Tyr's direction.

Reaching him in seconds, the God of Mischief folded himself elegantly onto the barstool next to his brother, resting his arms on the wooden bar. Invisible under the long-sleeved coat, Tyr happened to know those forearms, along with the god's chest, were decorated with black and gold Asgardian runes.

Knowing Loki, they were also likely tanned from the sun,

and adorned with significantly more expensive jewelry than Tyr's.

"Thank you for meeting me, brother," Loki said.

Something about the way Loki spoke always verged on dry humor, even sarcasm.

Tyr honestly couldn't always tell if his brother was being sincere. Rather than attempt to puzzle out the difference, he generally took Loki's words at face value.

"Of course," he said politely. "You said you have something for me, brother? Something important you wished to share?"

"Ah. Yes."

The God of Mischief dug his hand into the long coat he wore, and produced a small, black object with a silver connector.

"It was my wife's," Loki explained, placing it carefully down on the counter. "It was the last job she did for that horrible human who was blackmailing her. In Los Angeles."

Tyr nodded, frowning down at the object on the bar.

It was a human memory stick.

For a computer.

"What is on it?" Tyr said. "Can you tell me?"

Loki frowned, his hand and wrist rotating in a kind of vague shrug.

"She showed me," he said. "Lia. My wife. On one of her human machines. I didn't think to bring that device with me... but there were moving pictures." He made another flurry of gestures. "There was sound. It was a portion of some surveillance she did. In Nepal. Not long after we ran into one another."

It might have amused Tyr, in other times, that Loki himself was so clueless about the human technology he'd just handed him. Apparently, without his wife present, Loki had no idea how to show Tyr what was on the flash drive himself.

"My wife knows. If you require help—" Loki offered.

"I think I can manage, brother," Tyr said diplomatically. "But thank you. And thank your wife for me. I will call her, using a human telephone, if I require her help."

"You have our numbers?" Loki said. "Both of them? Here in Paris?"

"Yes."

"Ah. Good." Loki exhaled.

The God of Mischief combed his fingers through his longish, half-auburn hair, and Tyr again marveled at how perfect it looked.

Loki never did anything cheaply if he could pay top dollar.

"My wife was worried," the other god admitted. "I know you hardly owe me anything, brother, quite the opposite. But she was very worried, and given her condition, I thought of you. She seemed to think this could cause... problems. As in, *your* kind of problems."

Tyr nodded, frowning faintly.

"Tell your wife, she has my sincere thanks," Tyr said politely. "I appreciate you both including me. If you think it an area that might fall under my jurisdiction."

He paused then, quirking an eyebrow.

"Her condition?" he queried politely. "Then you and she—"

"Yes." Loki gave him a sideways look.

"Her idea? Or yours?"

"Mine, if you must know," Loki said, a little loftily. "But she was *entirely* onboard. So was our little ward." Loki's smile grew warmer, filled with obvious pride. "Our Maia is very much looking forward to a little sister or brother to boss around."

Seeing the heat rise to the other's eyes, Tyr smiled.

He patted his brother on the shoulder.

"I am very happy for you," he said sincerely. "It warms me greatly to see you so contented, Loki. More than I can say."

The other god seemed to relax.

Briefly, Tyr saw past the part of Loki that always seemed to be on guard—always ready to take advantage, to pull some kind of con, ready to evade or do battle, ready to lie or cheat or steal his way out of some difficult situation.

Behind that, Tyr's brother just seemed—happy.

"I *am* quite happy," the god admitted. "And feeling a bit possessive of that happiness, I confess." Loki gave him a worried look.

"You'll let me know, yes? If you need any assistance with this thing? My wife understands it far better than I. She used to work for this group, this 'Syndicate.' In fact, I arranged to more or less fake her death as far as they are concerned, so that we didn't have to worry about them bothering us again."

Sighing, he flicked his fingers towards the memory stick.

"As for what's on here, and why she wanted me to call *you,* all I can tell you is, she was doing surveillance at the instruction of her old boss. She only watched the recordings recently, after finding them in her bag... but what she saw concerned her. She tells me she pulled out the part she *particularly* wishes for you to see, and labeled it somehow inside here..."

Loki tapped the flash drive lightly with one finger, looking at the small piece of metal and circuits as if he was afraid it might explode.

Following Loki's finger with his eyes, Tyr only nodded.

"I am sure I can find it, brother. Thank you again. And thank Lia for me."

Loki looked up, his green eyes serious.

"I figure I owe you." A touch more reluctantly, he added, "...I figure I owe you *and* Thor. For speaking to father about me. For letting me keep my life here, and not separating me from my wife."

Tyr smiled, patting his brother's shoulder warmly.

"I see no debt between us, brother. Therefore, I view this as a gift." He gripped Loki's shoulder tighter. "And congratulations, brother. I am thrilled and moved to hear you will be adding to the family soon. Be sure and congratulate Lia for me, as well... and tell her I am very much looking forward to meeting my new niece or nephew."

Loki nodded.

There was a silence between them.

Somewhere in that silence, Loki seemed to decide their meeting was over.

Sliding off the barstool, the God of Mischief abruptly regained his feet. He stood there awkwardly for a beat, then thumped Tyr briskly on the back.

"Call us," he urged. "You are always welcome, brother. Thor said something about dinner one of these days, as well. With the wives. You should come, too."

Standing there a beat longer, Loki added,

"And call Lia if you need help with that... thing..."

Loki motioned vaguely at the flash drive he'd left on the wooden bar.

Tyr hid his smile politely.

"I will. And dinner sounds lovely. I would be most happy to come."

"Okay. I'll tell Thor."

Loki stood there, hands in his pockets.

Then, without another word, the god turned on his heel and walked away.

There was a flash of light when he opened the door to the street, letting in the afternoon sun.

Then Loki, God of Mischief, was gone.

WANT TO READ MORE?

Continue the rest of the novel:

TYR

(Gods on Earth #3)

Link: https://bit.ly/GOE03-eb

BOOKS IN THE GODS ON EARTH SERIES
(RECOMMENDED READING ORDER)

THOR (Book #1)
LOKI (Book #2)
TYR (Book #3)

❧

BOOKS IN THE VAMPIRE DETECTIVE MIDNIGHT SERIES
(RECOMMENDED READING ORDER)

VAMPIRE DETECTIVE MIDNIGHT (Book #1)
EYES OF ICE (Book #2)
THE PRESCIENT (Book #3)
FANG & METAL (Book #4)
THE WHITE DEATH (Book #5)

❧

BOOKS IN THE QUENTIN BLACK MYSTERY SERIES
(RECOMMENDED READING ORDER)

BLACK IN WHITE (Book #1)
Kirev's Door (Book #0.5)
BLACK AS NIGHT (Book #2)
Black Christmas (Book #2.5)
BLACK ON BLACK (Book #3)
Black Supper (Book #3.5)
BLACK IS BACK (Book #4)
BLACK AND BLUE (Book #5)
Black Blood (Book #5.5)
BLACK OF MOOD (Book #6)

BLACK TO DUST (Book #7)
IN BLACK WE TRUST (Book #8)
BLACK THE SUN (Book #9)
TO BLACK WITH LOVE (Book #10)
BLACK DREAMS (Book #11)
BLACK OF HEARTS (Book #12)
BLACK HAWAII (Book #13)

❧

BOOKS IN THE BRIDGE & SWORD SERIES - COMPLETE
(RECOMMENDED READING ORDER)

New York (Bridge & Sword Prequel Novel #0.5)
ROOK (Bridge & Sword #1)
SHIELD (Bridge & Sword #2)
SWORD (Bridge & Sword #3)
Revik (Bridge & Sword Prequel Novel #0.1)
SHADOW (Bridge & Sword #4)
KNIGHT (Bridge & Sword #5)
WAR (Bridge & Sword #6)
BRIDGE (Bridge & Sword #7)
Trickster (Bridge & Sword Prequel Novel #0.2)
The Defector (Bridge & Sword Prequel Novel #0.3)
PROPHET (Bridge & Sword #8)
A Glint of Light (Bridge & Sword #8.5)
DRAGON (Bridge & Sword #9)
The Guardian (Bridge & Sword #0.4)
SUN (Bridge & Sword #10)

❧

BOOKS IN THE ANGELS IN L.A. SERIES
(RECOMMENDED READING ORDER)

I, ANGEL (Book #1)
BAD ANGEL (Book #2)
FURY OF ANGELS (Book #3)
ANGEL ON FIRE (Book #4)

☙❦❧

Books in the Alien Apocalypse Series - COMPLETE
(Recommended Reading Order)

THE CULLING (Part I)
THE ROYALS (Part II)
THE NEW ORDER (Part III)
THE REBELLION (Part IV)
THE RINGS FIGHTER

JC Andrijeski is a *USA Today* and *Wall Street Journal* bestselling author who urban fantasy, paranormal romance and mysteries, and apocalyptic science fiction, often with a sexy and meta-physical bent.

JC has a background in journalism, history and politics, and has a tendency to traipse around the globe, eat odd foods, and read whatever she can get her hands on. She grew up in the Bay Area of California, but has lived abroad in Europe, Australia and Asia, and from coast to coast in the continental United States.

She currently lives and writes full time in Los Angeles.

facebook.com/JCAndrijeski
twitter.com/jcandrijeski
instagram.com/jcandrijeski
bookbub.com/authors/jc-andrijeski
amazon.com/JC-Andrijeski/e/Boo4MFTAPo

Printed in Great Britain
by Amazon

59507091R00128